"Daphne, look at me..."

Adam's voice was low and taut, intense with emotion as they swayed to the slow, soft music.

Daphne lifted her head and gazed at him. His eyes were blazing, a bright scorching blue. She saw longing there and something else—sexual desire. And as always, she felt herself melting.

"Yes," she said, answering his unspoken question. Her voice was little more than a sensual purr.

Adam stopped dancing, oblivious to the couples around them. "When?"

Heart beating, Daphne grasped his hand and turned to go. "Now. Please..."

Candace Schuler grew up in San Francisco, so it was only natural to set *Designing Woman* in that city. And like her heroine, Candace took part in many protests in her student days. That's as far as the similarity between them goes though, she acknowledges with a wink.

Candace currently lives in Dallas with her computer-consultant husband. She's working on her next Temptation, in which the heroine, Mike, runs a limo service.

Books by Candace Schuler
HARLEQUIN TEMPTATION
28–DESIRE'S CHILD

These books may be available at your local bookseller.

Don't miss any of our special offers. Write to us at the following address for information on our newest releases.

Harlequin Reader Service
901 Fuhrmann Blvd., P.O. Box 1397, Buffalo, NY 14240
Canadian address: P.O. Box 2800, Postal Station A,
5170 Yonge St., Willowdale, Ont. M2N 6J3

Designing Woman
CANDACE SCHULER

Harlequin Books

TORONTO • NEW YORK • LONDON
AMSTERDAM • PARIS • SYDNEY • HAMBURG
STOCKHOLM • ATHENS • TOKYO • MILAN

Published April 1986

ISBN 0-373-25202-1

Copyright © 1986 by Candace Schuler. All rights reserved.
Philippine copyright 1986. Australian copyright 1986.
Except for use in any review, the reproduction or utilization of
this work in whole or in part in any form by any electronic,
mechanical or other means, now known or hereafter invented,
including xerography, photocopying and recording, or in any
information storage or retrieval system, is forbidden without
the permission of the publisher, Harlequin Enterprises Limited,
225 Duncan Mill Road, Don Mills, Ontario, Canada M3B 3K9.

All the characters in this book have no existence outside the
imagination of the author and have no relation whatsoever to
anyone bearing the same name or names. They are not even
distantly inspired by any individual known or unknown to the
author, and all incidents are pure invention.

The Harlequin trademarks, consisting of the words, TEMPTATION,
HARLEQUIN TEMPTATION, HARLEQUIN TEMPTATIONS, and
the portrayal of a Harlequin, are trademarks of Harlequin Enterprises
Limited; the portrayal of a Harlequin is registered in the United
States Patent and Trademark Office and in the Canada Trade
Marks Office.

Printed in Canada

1

"NOW THAT'S WHAT I CALL a gorgeous man." Elaine Prescott, self-proclaimed connoisseur of men, tucked a strand of glossy brown hair behind one ear and turned from the gap in the stage curtains to address the room at large. "There's a tall blond hunk out there among all those doctors," she announced, raising her voice so that she could be heard above the noise of the models and technicians who scurried around the backstage area.

Several interested heads turned toward her but Daphne Granger's wasn't one of them. She was used to her assistant's frequent exclamations regarding the opposite sex and didn't even bother to look up from the loops of corded silk and colored glass beads that she was arranging around the waist of a volunteer model.

"Is he over six feet?" someone asked hopefully.

Daphne glanced up at that remark, smiling in spite of herself. The question had come from Suzie, one of the professional models. She had short, sleek, platinum blond hair, a figure that closely resembled a swizzle stick and stood an even six feet tall in her stockings.

Elaine peeked through the curtains again. "At least," she affirmed. "And he has shoulders like a football player. Great hair. Terrific tan," she reported, tossing the information back over her shoulder. "I can't see his eyes from here but they just have to be blue. Sensational smile. My God, I'd *die* if he smiled at me like that."

"Let me see." Suzie parted the curtains above Elaine's head. She whistled softly. "Six feet three, at least. I think I'm in love."

Daphne listened to them with only half an ear. She gave a final tweak to the belt she was arranging and stepped back, head tilted as she considered the effect. "You look terrific, Mrs. Danvers," she pronounced, smiling encouragingly at the nervous woman. "You'll knock 'em dead. Just don't sit down between now and the time you go on, okay?"

The woman nodded and walked stiffly to her place in the line of models, volunteer and professional, who were about to stage a charity fashion show for Children's Hospital of San Francisco.

Daphne had been roped into doing the fashion show by her oldest, best and most endearingly eccentric friend, Sunny McCorkle. Not that she minded doing it, of course, since the proceeds from the show were earmarked for new equipment for the hospital. And, besides, it was fun to be working on a worthy cause with Sunny again. It was almost like the old days when they had both been protesters on behalf of a cleaner environment, as well as sisters in the fight for equality of the sexes. And just like in the old days, Daphne worked in the background—or, in this case, the backstage—while Sunny held center court with a microphone in her hand, inciting the crowd to riot. Or whatever it was that one incited a group of distinguished doctors to do at a charity fashion show. Inciting them to buy, probably, Daphne decided with a grin.

Pulling her thoughts away from Sunny, she looked around for whatever else might need doing in these last few minutes before the show began. Her glance fell on Elaine and Suzie, giggling and whispering like a couple of sixteen-year-olds, their eyes still glued to the gap in the curtains. They looked, she thought, like Mutt and Jeff. Suzie, so tall and thin and ethereally blond, towered over the smaller, darker, more voluptuous Elaine as they peered out into the audience.

"Come on, you two, quit drooling all over the curtains and get to work. We're on in—" Daphne glanced at the slim gold watch on her wrist "—less than five minutes. And you haven't even got your dress on yet, Suzie," she accused, eyeing the model with mock ferocity. "Come on now." She clapped her hands together. "Move."

"But, Daphne, you haven't even looked yet," Elaine said teasingly, as she moved away from the curtains. "He's really gorgeous."

Daphne shrugged, displaying the smooth contours of one rounded shoulder as the wide boat neck of her silk dress slid downward. "He's probably gay," she said, picking up the clipboard that she had put down in order to help Mrs. Danvers with her belt. She reached up with one hand, absently adjusting the fallen neckline of her dress as she ran her eyes over the scribbled notes in front of her. "Half the men in San Francisco are gay."

"Oh, no. He can't be," Suzie wailed theatrically. "He's too tall."

"Tallness has nothing to do with it," Daphne said dryly. "Now go get dressed. And hurry."

"Humph! Easy for you to say." The lanky model grumbled good-naturedly as she moved toward the clothes rack. "You can date anybody. You're short."

"Five foot six is not short." Elaine defended her employer loyally. "Is it?" she added, looking to Daphne for confirmation.

"Not last I heard," Daphne mumbled, her mind already on other things. She didn't have time for all this nonsense. She shuffled through the papers attached to her clipboard. "Suzie, you go on third," she said, indicating the model's place in line with a flick of her hand. "Right behind Mrs. Garwood. Then Paula, Mrs. Ames, Heather." Daphne nodded at each woman in turn, a tiny frown of concentration between her arched brows. "Then Mrs. Danvers." She reached out to pat the woman's shoulder as she passed her. "You'll do fine," she said reassuringly. "Relax."

"Who goes on first?" someone asked.

Daphne glanced down at the clipboard and back up at the empty place in the line of beautifully dressed women in the silks and satins and glitter of evening wear. "Kali should be first in line." She looked around the room, but didn't spot the model in question. "Somebody tell Kali she's got thirty seconds to get here or I break every lovely bone in her body."

"I'm here, Daphne. Don't panic." A strikingly beautiful black woman, with skin the exact shade of polished African amber and enormous Kahlua-colored eyes, rushed to her place at the head of the line. The pale pink silk of her bat-winged dress billowed out behind her as she moved.

"Now when have you ever seen me panic?" Daphne looked up from her clipboard with a smile.

Kali pretended to consider, head tilted as she fastened a fan-shaped spray of pink tourmaline and diamonds to her ear. "That time that Elaine lost that whole trunk of silk flowers you wanted us to wear for the spring show at Neiman's."

"I did not lose them." Elaine, trailing behind Daphne like a loyal puppy, added her two cents to the conversation. "I merely misplaced them. And Daphne did not panic. She just, uh..."

"Came slightly unglued," Daphne put in, laughing. She cocked her head suddenly, holding one slim hand up for silence. The squeal of a microphone being adjusted was clearly audible. "Oh, damn! Sunny's announcing me already." Daphne thrust her clipboard in Elaine's direction.

"Just take a deep breath, Daphne," Elaine advised as she followed her employer to the edge of the curtain.

"Makeup okay?" Daphne tilted her beautifully made-up face to the light for inspection.

"Gorgeous," Elaine assured her honestly.

Daphne always looked gorgeous. There was no way that anyone with her cheekbones could be anything but gorgeous. That she also had wide golden-brown eyes, a delicately chiseled jawline and a neck like Audrey Hepburn didn't hurt, either.

"And my dress?" Daphne turned once, slowly, so that Elaine could make sure there were no straggling threads. The soft apricot silk evening dress with its wide boat neck and long, full sleeves gathered at the wrist with a narrow ring of crystal beads suited her warm peaches-and-cream skin to perfection. A corded belt of bright coral silk and more crystal beads accented the simple dress beautifully and set off a waist that was the envy of many of the models.

"The dress is lovely. Your hair looks great," Elaine said, eyeing the short, gently tousled hairdo approvingly. Daphne's baby-fine hair clung softly to her forehead and temples, leaving her ears and throat bare, with delicate, wavy tendrils that hugged the nape of her long, elegant neck. Its color was somewhere between aged bourbon and pale golden sherry; too dark to be called blonde but too bright to be labeled brown, either.

"Not a strand out of place," Elaine said, tweaking one of the soft curls. "Your notes are on the podium," she added, anticipating the next question. "Now, one more deep breath, and—" she put her hand in the small of Daphne's back "—you're on," she said, giving her employer a gentle push forward.

Daphne entered from stage right to polite applause and took her place at the podium. Surprisingly, Sunny didn't mouth any of the usual meaningless pleasantries that were appropriate to such an occasion. Instead, she simply gave Daphne's hand a reassuring squeeze, closed one huge chocolate-brown eye in a conspiratorial wink, and scampered off the stage before Daphne could so much as thank her for the lovely introduction.

Daphne thanked her anyway, then took another deep breath and smiled, willing the butterflies in her stomach to settle down. Although she would die before admitting to such a weakness, she really hated this part of a fashion show. She much preferred to manage things backstage and let her designs speak for themselves. Usually she did just that, but this was a charity function and the audience expected to see her.

"Good evening, everyone," she began, her naturally husky voice made even huskier by nervousness. The microphone squealed and Daphne backed away a little, eyeing it as if it might bite her. "I'm Daphne Granger and, as you all know, we're here tonight at the first annual Golden Gate Charity Fashion Show to benefit Children's Hospital," she said mechanically, staring straight ahead.

"Smile!" Elaine prompted from the wings.

Daphne smiled and remembered to look slowly from one side of the large room to the other so that everyone would feel as if she were talking to them personally.

"Tonight you'll be seeing some of the newest evening designs from my Night Lights collection. The gowns are being modeled both by professional models and by some of the lovely ladies of the Golden—" Daphne stopped suddenly in midspiel, her voice stuck somewhere in her throat.

Elaine's "gorgeous hunk"—it could be none other—was sitting at one of the first tables, almost directly in front of the podium. His eyes, just as blue as Elaine guessed they would be, were fastened intently on Daphne's face.

She blinked once and looked again, but he was still there. She shook her head slowly as if to clear her vision, causing her long crystal earrings to brush gently against her neck.

It can't be, she thought, her eyes wide with stunned surprise as she returned his stare. But she knew beyond a doubt that it was Adam—or someone who looked enough like him to be his twin.

No wonder Sunny had been in such a hurry to get off the stage! She had known he was going to be here. She had probably invited him. The traitor!

"Daphne!" She heard Elaine hiss at her from the wings.

"Some...uh, some of the ladies of the Golden Gate fundraising committee will also model tonight." Daphne mumbled the words into the microphone and then paused, unable to think of what came next while Adam sat there, staring at her with that astonished look on his face. She averted her eyes, tearing them away from Adam's with difficulty, and tried vainly to remember the rest of her opening speech. But even with the little three by five cue cards that Elaine had made for her she couldn't remember what she was supposed to say.

What is he doing here, she wondered frantically. He was supposed to be working at a hospital in Los Angeles. Hadn't Sunny told her, oh, years ago it seemed, that he had done his residency at some hospital down there? What was he doing in San Francisco at a Children's Hospital charity function?

"Daph-nee!" Elaine's voice was urgent now.

Daphne glanced toward stage right, her eyes focusing blindly on her agitated assistant. "And, uh, now," she improvised, "here to describe the fashions you'll be seeing tonight is my very capable and, uh, lovely assistant, Elaine Prescott." She motioned for the other woman to join her at the podium. "Elaine?"

Putting down her clipboard, Elaine hurried out onto the stage, her hands unconsciously fluffing up the low-cut ruffled neckline of her yellow crepe de chine gown as she moved. "What happened?" she whispered, automatically smiling at the crowd as Daphne introduced her again.

Daphne shrugged, miming confusion as she turned away from the audience, and thrust the cue cards into Elaine's hands. Then she walked, as fast as was possible without actually running, toward the safety of backstage.

"Daphne, are you all right?" Suzie, resplendent now in ice-blue chiffon and drop-dead sapphires, was the first to reach her.

"What happened?" Kali's concerned voice rose above the others.

"Where's Sunny?" Daphne demanded, ignoring the questions. "I want to wring her neck."

"Huh?"

"The tall busty redhead in the gold lamé," Daphne elaborated, looking around for her intended victim. "Looks like she stuck her finger in a light socket," she added unkindly.

"Oh, Mrs. McCorkle. She went that way." Kali pointed toward the backstage exit. "Fast."

"Coward!" Daphne muttered to herself, her eyes on the neon exit sign. Then she turned, glaring at the models who clustered around her. "Why are you all just standing around? You're supposed to be doing a fashion show."

"But, Daphne—"

"You're on, Kali," she instructed, nodding her head toward the stage.

The black woman instantly assumed the haughty, elegant expression of the professional runway model and glided out onto the stage. She paused as the spotlight hit her, raising her arms to show off the wide bat-wing sleeves of the dress, and then undulated down the walk with her arms still held high so that the soft pink silk billowed as she moved. She paused at the end of the runway, twirled once, very slowly, and started back toward the stage.

"Our next model this evening is Mrs. Beth Garwood, the wife of Dr. Arthur Garwood. She's wearing a gold shot chemise dress..." Elaine's voice was well modulated and professional but Daphne barely heard it.

She peered around the edge of the curtain, her eyes drawn irresistibly to the table where Adam sat. His golden blond hair seemed to catch and reflect the spotlight that followed the models up and down the runway, making him easy to pick out. Dr. Brian McCorkle, Sunny's husband, was at the same table. The seat between the two men, Sunny's seat, was empty. Proving decisively, Daphne thought, that her so-called best friend had engineered the whole thing!

Suddenly, as if feeling her eyes upon him, Adam half turned in his chair and looked back over his shoulder. There was a puzzled expression on his handsome face as he stared toward the spot where Daphne had disappeared into the curtains, as if he couldn't believe what he had seen, either. Daphne hastily tucked herself further behind the concealing material, all thoughts of her traitorous friend flying from her mind.

He still looked the same, she thought, daring to peek again after a minute. Oh, he was older, of course. Who wasn't? But the lines of age and experience etched in his face were infinitely more interesting and attractive than the innocent, aw-shucks, farmboy face he had had as a younger man.

His hair hadn't changed at all. It was still thick and straight and the color of ripe, golden wheat. "Great hair," as Elaine had said. He wore it shorter now, but that stubborn cowlick still fell over his forehead. And he still used the same impatient gesture when he pushed it back, she noted.

From what she could see, he had managed to keep the physique of his younger years, too. He still looked more like the football player that Elaine had tagged him than a successful doctor. Doctors, Daphne thought whimsically, a ghost of a smile curving her full coral-tinted lips, shouldn't be allowed to have shoulders like that. Or, if they did, they shouldn't be allowed to wear tuxedos.

It was those shoulders and that still magnificent build that had first attracted her to him. He had just been coming out of the entrance of Harding Park, near the university, clad in battered running shoes and a pair of faded blue shorts. A sweat-soaked terry headband had held his hair out of his face, and there was a gleam of hard physical exertion covering his body.

She remembered vividly how the muscles of his arms and shoulders rippled in the late afternoon sunlight. His legs were long and lean—like a runner's should be—with powerful, well-developed thigh and calf muscles that seemed to move effortlessly as he jogged out of the park. Fine, downy, blond hair glinted over his legs and forearms and the wide expanse of his chest, giving him an all over golden glow. He was as beautiful as a young Greek god and Daphne had been so enthralled by the sheer male beauty of him that she forgot to pay attention to what she was doing and ran into him with her bicycle.

Lord, but he had been angry! For the first few minutes, anyway. She had, after all, knocked him down and left tread marks across the toe of his right sneaker. It had taken half a dozen apologetic smiles and the promise of a date before he was willing to forgive her.

Daphne sighed and moved back behind the curtain. Where had all the time gone? It seemed like only yesterday that Adam had been an intensely dedicated, nose-to-the-grindstone young med student and she had been his unlikely girlfriend; an impulsive, emotional young woman who protested on behalf of what she considered the unfortunates in the world and dreamed of becoming a fashion designer.

Adam will be thirty-seven in a couple of weeks, she thought, recalling his birthday without effort. *I turned thirty-one this year.* And in just two months it would be eleven years since their divorce.

"Daphne, what happened out there?" Suzie had changed into her second outfit, a slim one-shoulder column of sleek satin that almost matched her platinum hair, and was waiting for her cue to go on again. She put her hand on Daphne's arm. "Are you all right? You look like you've seen a ghost."

Daphne smiled a little wryly and patted the hand on her sleeve. "I guess I have, sort of." She nodded toward the audience. "See that blond hunk of yours out there?"

Suzie peeked around the curtain. "Uh-huh. He's sitting at the first table." She licked her lips. "Yummy."

"He's my ex-husband."

The model's head snapped around. "Your ex-husband? Really?" She looked out toward the audience again, amazement in her wide blue eyes. "The hunk is your ex-husband?"

"What's the matter? Don't you think I could be married to a man like that?" Daphne said, her voice only half teasing. She had gotten that kind of reaction before. People had found it hard to believe that a serious, dedicated medical student like Adam Forrest could be married to the emotional, impulsive girl that she had been at that time in her life.

"I didn't mean it like that. It's just that, well—" Suzie shrugged her fashionably thin shoulders "—I didn't know you'd ever been married to anyone besides Miles." Her look became frankly curious. "You must have been awfully young that first time around."

"I was eighteen when we got married," Daphne said softly, thinking suddenly of the way they had eloped.

It had been her idea, their elopement. She had talked herself blue in the face, trying to convince him that it was the best thing to do. But Adam wanted to do the sensible thing; he wanted to wait until they could "afford" to get married, until he was out of med school and into his internship, at least, before taking on the responsibility of a wife. But Daphne didn't want to wait. She couldn't. And, in the end, neither could he.

Maybe it would have been better if they had waited, she thought. Maybe they would still be married now if she had allowed Adam to do the sensible thing. Who knows? But it was too late now. It had been too late eleven years ago.

"I was twenty when he filed for divorce," she added softly, almost to herself. There was a wealth of sadness in the words.

"Oh." Suzie obviously didn't know what to say to that. "Gee, I'm sorry, Daphne."

"Oh, don't be." Daphne shook herself out of her reverie. "It was a long time ago."

"Did you know he was going to be here tonight?"

Daphne shook her head. "I'd heard that he was doing his residency in plastic surgery at some hospital in L.A." She shrugged and the shoulder of her dress slipped downward again. She didn't notice. "But that was, oh, five or six years ago, I guess. So I suppose I should have considered the fact that he'd probably be back in the Bay Area by now. He always said that he intended to establish his practice in San

Francisco." She sighed softly. "Well, that's neither here nor there." She lifted her small chin decisively. "I've got a fashion show to do."

She moved away from the curtain then and picked up the clipboard from the stool where Elaine had placed it when she went onstage. Walking briskly, she headed toward the clothes rack, her mind determinedly on the business at hand.

"You have one more dress after that, right, Suzie?" she said over her shoulder.

The model nodded. "Yes."

"Okay, listen up, everybody." Daphne raised her voice slightly as she addressed the models who were bouncing around backstage, struggling in and out of clothes. "As soon as you've all shown your last dress, then it's everybody on stage for the finale, okay?"

She turned to watch Suzie parade out onto the stage. The tall, lanky model seemed to float down the runway, long silver ribbons fluttering from her right shoulder as she moved.

"And that, ladies and gentlemen, concludes our fashion show for this evening," Elaine said as the final model slowly made her way back up the length of the runway. "What do you say we give a big round of applause to our lovely models?" she continued as they all began to file out for the finale, filling the runway with a dazzling kaleidoscope of fabric and color.

"Let's get the designer of these fabulous clothes out here, too, shall we?" Elaine went on.

Daphne had known the words were coming, they always did when Elaine did the commentary for a show, but she wished, just this once, that her assistant wasn't so eager to give credit where credit was due.

"Our Daphne seems to be a little shy tonight," Elaine said, smiling at the audience as she deliberately ignored Daphne's hand signals. "Let's see if we can persuade her to come on out and take a bow." She turned toward the wing where Daphne was standing, adding her applause to that of the audience.

Daphne fixed her assistant with a threatening glare and then, pasting a wide smile on her face, walked out onto the stage. Very deliberately, she forced herself not to look at the table where she knew Adam was sitting as she stepped up to the podium.

"Thank you, ladies and gentlemen," she said, when the applause had died down. "I hope you enjoyed the fashion show this evening. I know we enjoyed putting it on for you." She paused, smiling warmly as the applause began again, and her eyes were irresistibly drawn to Adam's table.

His golden head was tilted slightly to the right as he gazed up at her and there was the hint of a question in his pose. And then he raised his glass and smiled. It was that sweet, slow, utterly charming smile that she remembered far too well for her own good.

Daphne felt her knees turn to mush and it was all she could do to finish her little speech and get off the stage without falling down.

2

IT WAS CHAOS BACKSTAGE. Technicians went about the business of packing up their equipment, stoically dodging around the models who scurried back and forth in various stages of undress as they struggled to get out of their borrowed finery and into the gowns they would wear for the rest of the evening's festivities. There was a high-society charity dance being held in one of the hotel ballrooms to which they had all been invited.

It was easy to tell the pros from the amateurs. The doctors' wives were all huddled behind a curtained-off partition as they changed, while the professional models, used to displaying their bodies before the eyes of both man and camera, changed anywhere there was room. They created privacy simply by turning their backs.

"Hey, Daphne." Elaine hurried up to her employer, her voice several octaves higher than usual in her excitement. Her glossy brown bob swirled around her face as she moved, revealing glimpses of the large baroque pearls that adorned her ears. "Suzie just told me the most *amazing* thing."

"I'll just bet she did," Daphne said dryly as she continued to match the dresses, which had been hung haphazardly on the metal clothes rack, against the list attached to her ever-present clipboard.

"Well," Elaine prodded, hazel eyes wide with curiosity. "Is it true?"

"Is what true?" Daphne didn't look up. *Maybe if I ignore her*, she thought, *she'll go away*.

"Is that gorgeous blond hunk really your ex-husband?"

"Modesty forbids me to comment on the 'gorgeous' part," said a warm, masculine voice from behind them. "But I *am* her ex-husband." Daphne didn't turn around but she knew he was smiling. She could hear it in his voice. "That is, if this elegant lady is the same Daphne who used to wear bell-bottom jeans and homemade tie-dye T-shirts."

"Tie-dye T-shirts? Daphne?" Elaine's eyes got even wider, her head bobbing back and forth as she tried to look at both Daphne and the "gorgeous hunk" at the same time. "You've got to be kidding."

"He isn't." Daphne spoke up before Adam could reply. "Believe it or not, those T-shirts were among my very first efforts at design." She put her clipboard down on a nearby chair and turned around to face the man who had once been her husband. "Hello, Adam."

"Hello, Daffy," he said, calling her by that ridiculous nickname that no one else had ever dared use. "It's been a long time."

"Yes," she agreed, because she could think of nothing else to say. It had been a long time.

And yet, Daphne felt as if it hadn't been any time at all. He was having the same effect on her that he'd always had. Just the sight of him, close up like this, was doing strange things to her heartbeat. But what else had she expected? She had never, not once in the past eleven years, ever stopped loving him. Not even when she was married to Miles.

They stood there, silently staring at each other, seemingly oblivious to the models and stagehands swarming around them. They didn't even seem to be aware of Elaine, standing wide-eyed with admiration and ill-concealed curiosity by Daphne's elbow.

"So," he said softly, reaching out to gently grasp her shoulders. The neckline of her dress had fallen to one side again and his hand made direct contact with her warm flesh. Daphne could feel the separate imprint of each long finger curving around the delicate bones of her shoulder.

Such gentle hands, she thought. And then she remembered. He had always had gentle hands, big as a linebacker's but infinitely gentle. Infinitely skillful. Indisputably the hands of a surgeon.

"Let me look at you." He held her away from him as his eyes ran over her assessingly from the top of her elegantly tousled head to the toes of her bare strappy evening shoes, and back up again. "You cut your hair."

Whatever she had expected him to say, it hadn't been that. Cutting her previously waist-length hair had been the least of the changes she had made.

"Yes," she said again. Her hand fluttered to the back of her neck, fingering the soft, clinging tendrils and then, before she stopped to think about it, she reached up and touched the thick lock of blond hair that fell over his forehead. "So did you," she said, smoothing it back with a proprietary, almost wifely gesture.

She didn't seem to hear his swift intake of breath at her gentle, careless caress.

Wonderingly, she touched the tiny crow's feet at the corner of his left eye. Her fingers whispered over one of the twin creases that ran from nose to mouth in either lean cheek. His lips were thinner, harder than they had been in his youth, she thought as she continued taking inventory. They had lost that look of vulnerability and sweet sensuality. He had the mouth of a virile, passionate man now; he looked experienced and knowing.

An infinitely more interesting face, Daphne thought again, marveling at the healthy, golden glow of his skin. He looked as much like a Greek god as he ever had, only more so. He reminded her of a mature and rugged Apollo, all big and golden and glowing with health.

Suddenly, Daphne became aware of what she was doing. Her hand dropped abruptly to her side, and almost without conscious thought she slipped into the character that she had so deftly learned to play.

"I'm forgetting my manners," she said, drawing her composure around her like a shawl. She took a small step backward and his hands dropped from her shoulders. Daphne adjusted the neckline of her dress, covering the place where his fingers had been.

"Adam, this is my assistant, Elaine Prescott." She turned toward Elaine who still stood, gaping, at her elbow. "Elaine, this 'gorgeous hunk'—" her eyebrows arched slightly when Elaine actually had the grace to blush "—is Dr. Adam Forrest."

"Dr. Forrest." Elaine bobbed her head in greeting, holding out a slim hand as she looked up at him through her lashes.

"Call me Adam, please." He smiled at her, and her blush deepened.

"Adam," she echoed, bobbing her head again as he released her hand.

Daphne blinked, amazed. Was this blushing schoolgirl the same Elaine who whistled at construction workers?

"Will we see you at the charity dance tonight?" Adam said to the younger woman.

"Not if she doesn't get busy now, you won't." Daphne broke into the conversation when Elaine just continued to stand there staring. "I want these dresses covered before we leave," she continued. "And all the jewelry collected and put into the hotel safe. Elaine?" She waved her hand in front of her assistant's face. "Earth to Elaine. Come in, please."

Elaine's eyes refocused. "What? Oh, the dresses. Sure. I'll do it right now." She smiled up at Adam one more time before she turned to go, and her usual brand of brashness seemed to come back to her. "Save me a dance, okay, gorgeous?" she quipped, bouncing away.

Adam laughed, shaking his head in disbelief. "Is she always like that?"

"Oh, no." Daphne's voice and expression were deadpan. "She's just shy because she doesn't know you yet. Wait until she gets warmed up."

"No thanks. I think I'll pass." He sighed, raking one hand through the lock of hair that had fallen across his forehead. "A kid like that makes me feel about a hundred years old."

"Well, you *have* gotten older," Daphne agreed.

Adam's eyes narrowed slightly, trying to decide whether she was teasing or not.

"I mean that as a compliment," she added. "Experience looks good on you."

"On you, too." He smiled and his bright blue eyes ran over her again, briefly, but with more masculine appraisal than the last time. "You're even more beautiful than I remembered."

A faint smile curved Daphne's lips. Compliments from the closemouthed Adam, she thought, and delivered with such confidence, too. Experience had apparently given him more than just an interesting face. He had never called her beautiful before, except in bed. Words had always been hard for Adam.

"Why, Adam," she said lightly, teasingly, a slight smile still hovering on her lips. "I didn't know you noticed such things."

He grinned in acknowledgment of her gentle barb and made a slight movement with his hand, as if he wanted to touch her again. Apparently he thought better of it because, instead of touching her, he stuffed his hands into the pants pockets of his tuxedo.

The movement pushed his jacket back, exposing the pristine elegance of his white dress shirt with its fine pintuck pleating and dashing wing-tip collar. His bow tie nestled like a black satin butterfly at the base of his strong golden throat, and the cummerbund around his lean waist was a deep wine red that emphasized the truly awesome broadness of his chest above it and the narrowness of the hips below.

He had always been tall and handsome, but when, she wondered, had he gotten so elegant? So devastatingly sophisticated?

"Are you coming to this charity dance?" he said easily, trying for casualness as he leaned one broad shoulder against the wall.

"I haven't decided yet." Daphne's husky voice was equally casual, belying the sudden quivering of her stomach. He looked like an ad for some swanky men's cologne, she thought, staring at him with a slightly bemused expression on her face. But how he'd hate to have her tell him that. Receiving compliments had always been as hard for Adam as giving them. He used to blush like a schoolboy when she called him her Greek god.

Would he still blush, she wondered.

"What's to decide?" Adam's voice broke into her thoughts. "Your assistant there—" he glanced in Elaine's direction "—is packing all this up for you, isn't she?"

Daphne nodded. "But I should be here to oversee things."

Adam shook his head. "No excuses." He smiled that sleepy, inviting smile of his. "We could have a dance for old time's sake. It'll be fun."

"Well . . ." Daphne hesitated. It would be more than just fun, it would be . . . what? Exciting? Thrilling?

Try dangerous, she thought, dangerous and foolish. He still had the power to stir her deepest emotions. Just standing here with him had more than proved that to her. Dancing with him would be fatal. Still, she thought, why not? What could it hurt? She wasn't married anymore...but was he?

Her eyes flickered to his left hand. There was no ring but that didn't prove anything. Neither of them had worn a ring when they'd been married, partly because of her blossoming women's lib philosophy and partly because they couldn't afford it.

"Won't your wife object to all these free dances you're passing out?" she said, before she could stop herself.

Adam's eyes captured hers. "I'm not married." There was a brief pause as he tried to read the expression in her big golden-brown eyes. "Are you?" he asked, very carefully.

Daphne shook her head slowly. "Not anymore." She glanced downward. "I was, but Miles—" She moved her shoulders uneasily and the neckline of her dress slid down again. "My husband died three years ago."

"I should say I'm sorry, shouldn't I?" Adam reached out and lifted her chin, bringing her eyes up to his again. Daphne felt his touch sizzle down to her toes. "But I'd be lying."

"Lying?" Daphne echoed.

"I make it a rule never to make love to married women," he explained softly. "And I've suddenly discovered that I want, very much, to make love to you."

"Oh." The single word came out as a breathless, throaty whisper. This new, older, more experienced Adam was certainly full of surprises, she thought. The Adam she had known all those years ago would never have said anything like that, especially not in a room full of people.

"Oh, indeed," he said, his gentle smile mocking both of them. His hand moved from her chin to feather lightly down the slim column of her long, elegant neck. It settled on her bare shoulder again. Daphne shivered and the quivery feeling in her stomach spread lower. "Well?"

"Well?" she murmured.

"Am I going to make love to you? With you?" His voice was a husky whisper.

Where had he learned all this, she wondered a bit frantically. His new technique was devastating. Straight to the point and utterly, utterly devastating.

"But I thought..." She made a vague, fluttering gesture with one hand. "The charity dance, aren't you supposed to be there?" In her suddenly flustered state it didn't even occur to her that he didn't mean—couldn't possibly mean—that he wanted to make love to her *now*, right this instant.

Adam shrugged and Daphne's eyes followed the movement, mesmerized by the way the fine black material of his tuxedo jacket strained against his broad shoulders. "There are over three-hundred people in the ballroom." He caressed her shoulder lightly, his thumb massaging the tender hollow of her throat. "They'd never miss me."

"Don't you have a date or—" she lifted the shoulder that he wasn't touching "—or something?"

Adam shook his head. "I came with a large group of people," he told her. "The fashion show was merely a duty appearance for charity." He grinned. "Actually, Sunny threatened to picket my office if I didn't come. Now, any more excuses?" His voice was gently teasing.

"I have to supervise things here. No, really," she added when he started to interrupt. "There's a fortune in jewelry that has to go in the hotel safe." She paused, her eyes meeting his for the barest instant. "Insurance won't cover it if I keep it in my room."

Adam's hand stilled on her shoulder and a tiny spark seemed to flare in the depth of his eyes, making them an even brighter, deeper blue. Daphne recognized that look instantly. Desire. The same feeling was racing madly through her own body.

"You're staying at the hotel?" The words seemed to rasp out of his throat.

"Yes," she said, low. "I always stay here when I'm in town, which is every few months or so. More often, lately. I seem to pick up more and more clients, buyers, in this area every season." She knew she was babbling, but she couldn't seem to stop. "Business is getting so good, I've been seriously thinking of opening up a West Coast office. It would—"

"Daffy." His fingers tightened on her shoulder, silencing her. "When I said I wanted to make love to you, I didn't mean that I was going to throw you down and ravish you the minute we're alone, you know."

Her eyes grew wide. "You didn't?" she said softly, wondering if she sounded as disappointed as she felt.

Adam uttered a strangled sound, halfway between a chuckle and a groan. "No, I didn't." His free hand came up to grasp her other shoulder gently. "Although, believe me, I'd like to," he said ruefully. "But I also like to think that I've developed more finesse than that. Besides, I'm not so thickheaded that I can't see the idea scares you."

"Oh, no. It—" Daphne began and then stopped abruptly, lowering her head to hide the light blush that touched her cheeks. She had given too much away already.

"All right, it doesn't exactly scare you," he amended. "But it makes you a little nervous, right?"

Daphne nodded.

"Well, it makes me a little nervous, too. Hell, it makes me a lot nervous! It's been quite a shock seeing you again like this without—" he paused as if searching for a word

"—without any warning. I had no idea that tonight's fashion guru and my ex-wife were one and the same. And I certainly didn't expect to still feel—" He broke off abruptly and his hands dropped from her shoulders. He shoved them back into his pockets and half turned away from her, his eyes following a crack in the floor. "I didn't realize that you'd have such a strong effect on me." He looked up at her then, a sheepish, almost embarrassed expression on his face. "But I'm as hot for you right now as I was that first time you ran over me with your bicycle," he admitted, his eyes blazing into hers. He was blushing under his tan.

"Adam!" she said softly, incredulously. She didn't know what else to say. It was how she felt, too, but she'd had the advantage, however slight, of *knowing* that's the way she would feel if she ever saw him again. She had always known it. It had obviously come as quite a surprise to him.

"Daphne!" He mimicked her shocked tone, a self-mocking light in his eyes as he stared back at her. Then he shrugged and his chest lifted in a deep sigh. "Maybe we should just forget that...dance," he said, looking away from her again. The blush had receded, leaving his face smooth and golden and, she thought, a bit strained. "It was a bad idea, anyway. It's probably better to let sleeping dogs lie." He ran his hand through his hair and turned as if to leave.

"I was sort of looking forward to it," Daphne murmured, without specifying exactly what "it" was. Her husky voice was tinged with disappointment.

Adam paused. "So was I," he said softly, "but—"

Daphne could see the struggle on his face, could see him warring with himself over what he should do and what he wanted to do. The struggle took less than ten seconds.

"All right," he said with the air of a man casting caution and good sense to the wind. "We'll have that dance. And then maybe we'll go somewhere quiet for a drink. Talk about old times and catch up with each other's lives. How does that sound to you?"

Daphne nodded her approval. "Sounds fine."

"All right, then. Why don't you do whatever it is you have to do and I'll meet you in the main lobby in, say—" he glanced at his watch "—thirty minutes?"

Unconsciously, Daphne followed the direction of his gaze, but it wasn't the watch that caught her attention. It was the fine blond hairs sprinkled across his wrist and over the back of his hand that held her eyes. They glinted like gold against his tanned skin.

The hair on his chest was like that, she remembered suddenly, fine and golden and as soft as silk against the palm of her hand... or against her breasts.

"Is that enough time?"

"What?" Daphne looked up, her eyes soft and slightly unfocused. "Oh, the time," she murmured inanely, a slight blush of her own coloring her cheeks. She hoped fervently that he hadn't added mind reading to his list of new talents. "Yes, that's plenty of time." It wasn't, of course—an hour would be more like it—but Daphne was hardly aware of what she was saying.

"Thirty minutes, then." Adam hesitated for the barest instant, indecision on his face, and then he cupped Daphne's cheek in his palm and bent his head, touching his lips lightly to hers.

Taken by surprise, Daphne responded as naturally as if there hadn't been eleven years between this kiss and the last one they had shared. Her head tilted back, her eyes closed, her lips parted on a little sigh, and what Adam had intended as a brief, experimental meeting of lips turned into something more.

He took fire immediately, goaded by Daphne's half sigh and her instinctive acquiescence. His hand moved from her cheek to the nape of her neck, sliding around the curve of her long elegant throat, causing her crystal earrings to bounce gently against the back of his hand. He molded his palm to the base of her skull, splaying his fingers through her pale golden-brown hair, and tilted her head to one side, angling his own so that he could take full possession of her willing mouth.

They stood like that for a few endless seconds, connected only by the heat of their clinging mouths and his hand at the back of her head. Their bodies seemed to sway toward each other without actually touching, like a pair of cobras weaving in unison to the sound of the magician's flute.

It was Adam who broke the kiss. He lifted his head slightly, tearing his mouth from hers with difficulty, and pulled back to look down into her face. His eyes had the heavy-lidded, sleepy expression that Daphne recognized immediately as a sign of his desire. Her own eyes, she knew, had probably lightened to gold as they always did when she was aroused.

"Don't keep me waiting, Daffy," Adam said then, almost pleadingly. His lips still hovered a mere sigh away from hers. His breathing was rapid, his cheeks flushed.

Daphne shook her head, unable to form a coherent thought, let alone give voice to one. "Waiting?" she said breathlessly.

"In the lobby." He brushed his lips softly across hers once . . . twice . . . as his hand cradled the back of her head. "I'll be waiting for you in the main lobby, near the entrance to the ballroom," he whispered against her mouth. Then, reluctantly, he straightened away from her and his eyes drifted past her shoulder for just a second.

Behind Daphne, standing with their collective mouths hanging open, were five or six models and Elaine Prescott. Elaine winked.

The slight, passion-induced flush on Adam's clean shaven cheeks deepened and spread over his entire face, turning it a fiery red. His hand dropped from the back of Daphne's neck. "Thirty minutes," he said tersely, and then he turned on his heel and strode, stiff-backed, toward the exit.

"My, oh, my." Elaine's whisper rose, sotto voce, into the small, sudden silence that Adam had left behind him. "Doesn't he just make your heart go pitty-pat?" she said to no one in particular.

Daphne turned around to face the group of grinning women standing behind her. "Don't you ladies have anything better to do?" she snapped, unaware that the soft look on her face made her words less forceful than she had intended. Still, they were quite forceful enough to make the models who didn't know her well begin to shuffle away. "Like getting yourselves ready for that charity shindig?"

"I am ready," Elaine started to defend herself. "All I have to do is freshen my—"

"Good." With an abrupt movement, Daphne turned and snatched up her clipboard. She thrust it into Elaine's hands, pointedly ignoring the two models who hadn't slunk off with the others. "Then you have plenty of time to see that everything is in order before you go to the dance."

"But, Daphne." Surprised by her employer's highly unusual behavior, Elaine couldn't even form a proper protest.

Usually, it was Daphne who saw to all the details at the end of the show, making sure that all the clothes and shoes and accessories that had been used were accounted for. And usually, it was Daphne who saw to it that each model, especially the volunteers, had been personally complimented and thanked for her part in the fashion show. Usually, Daphne was the last one to leave. But not tonight.

"Make sure that the jewelry is put back in the safe," she instructed Elaine. "And get an itemized receipt for it from the hotel manager," she added over her shoulder as she headed for the exit.

"But Daphne," Elaine said again, too late. Daphne was already gone. Elaine looked at the two models who still stood near her, shrugging her shoulders when Kali raised a questioning eyebrow.

"Ex-husband," Suzie said succinctly, as if that explained everything.

3

AS MUCH AS SHE HAD SURPRISED Elaine with her behavior, Daphne had surprised herself even more. Walking out, with all the final chores of a fashion show still unattended to, was as unlike her as . . . as standing on her head in the middle of Times Square!

It was one thing, she realized, to know that you were still in love with your ex-husband with eleven years and three thousand miles between you. It was quite another to be suddenly confronted with the living, breathing, breathtaking reality of the man, especially when you weren't prepared for it. It tended to put things in a whole different perspective.

Daphne stood in front of the bathroom mirror in her hotel room, lipstick pencil in hand, trying to figure out just what that perspective was—and failing miserably. She could only seem to think of one thing.

I'm as hot for you right now as I was that first time you ran over me with your bicycle. Had Adam really said that? And had he meant it?

"Oh, God, I hope so," Daphne said out loud, surprising herself with the fervent sound of her voice. A rueful, self-mocking smile twisted her lips as she met her eyes in the mirror. "Fool," she said to her reflection. "You're an idiot to even *think* of going to bed with him. The man divorced you, remember?"

She remembered—vividly. She would never forget it as long as she lived, but it didn't seem to make any difference. She had only to look at Adam and all the old feelings rushed back. No matter what he had done she wanted him. She always had and always would.

"Fool," she said again but the word lacked conviction. She could still feel his lips on hers. They tasted exactly as she remembered: hot, sweet, passionate, possessive.

She closed her eyes as the memories assailed her. The last—the final—time Adam had kissed her, had loved her, was as clear in her mind as if it had been yesterday instead of eleven years ago. It had been the night before she was to leave for New York and Adam's lovemaking had been tinged with a barely controlled anger because he didn't want her to go.

"You can design clothes right here in San Francisco," he'd argued. "You *are* designing clothes here. Why do you have to run off to New York?"

She'd tried to explain it to him; a big-name department store had expressed an interest in her designs and she was flying back East to pursue the matter. She'd only be gone for a month or two at the most. Why couldn't he understand? Her career was as important to her as his was to him, despite the fact that she only cut and sewed on fabric instead of human bodies.

"Think of the money this could mean," she said finally, knowing that it might be the one thing that could reconcile Adam to her going. The money didn't really mean much to her, but Adam hated being poor. He had been poor all his life and it kept him from doing the things he wanted to do for his family, and for her. "I could make lots of money, if they really like my designs. We could move out of this dinky apartment. You could quit driving that taxi and give all your time to your studies."

But, surprisingly, Adam wasn't swayed. In fact, the mention of money only seemed to make him more set against her going. The argument had come to an abrupt halt when he had become impatient, and thus inarticulate, with the angry words they were flinging at each other. With a strangled oath, he had grabbed her, kissing her into silence, covering her body with his as they sank to the floor of their tiny studio apartment.

Their arguments always ended that way. In bed, with Daphne whimpering and writhing beneath the heated thrust of his golden body, willing to forget her side of the argument and give in. But this time it was too important to her and she couldn't—wouldn't—give in to the magic of his gentle, skillful hands and avid mouth.

The next morning she had been on that plane for New York. Her ticket, paid for by the department store, was round-trip but the return date had been left open. She had never used it because, one month later, Adam had filed for divorce, charging her with desertion.

Daphne opened her eyes and stared at herself in the bathroom mirror, feeling a sudden surge of the same anger, the same hurt that she had felt then. The lip pencil she held poised halfway to her mouth fell from her hand and her fingers clutched the edge of the basin, the long coral nails vivid against the white porcelain, as all the painful memories rushed back.

The bastard had divorced her! Just like that. Without a phone call, without a letter, he'd handled it all through a lawyer. In typical tight-lipped silence, Adam had ended their marriage without so much as another word between them. And Daphne, incredulous and hurt but as stubborn as he, had let him.

And now he has the gall to think that I'm going to fall into bed with him, as if nothing had happened!

He had acted almost as if he wasn't aware of the eleven years that had passed since the last time they'd seen each other. Did he really think she was going to let him make love to her? Just like that? After the way he had broken her heart and shattered her life? After no word, not even a lousy Christmas card, in eleven years? After...

Obviously, he did think that. Because she had let him think it. Because, she admitted, forcing herself to be honest, *she* had thought it, too. For one crazy, completely insane minute she had actually contemplated going to bed with her ex-husband.

And was still contemplating it.

Sighing, she picked up her lip pencil from the far corner of the bathroom counter where it had rolled when she dropped it. With careful strokes she finished outlining her mouth, filling in the color with a matching soft coral lipstick. Then, quite unnecessarily, she touched up her eye makeup: darkening and smudging the soft brown liner, dusting on more gilded ivory highlighter just under her brows and adding another coat of mascara to her lashes.

She tilted her head consideringly. The woman who stared back at her was chic, elegant and sophisticated—light years removed from the long-haired, jean-clad girl she had been. At least on the outside. Inside, though...inside she was the same lovesick idiot that she had always been where Adam was concerned.

"If you had any sense at all," she said to her reflection, "you'd lock yourself in this room and forget you ever saw him tonight."

Obviously, though, she didn't have any sense. With another resigned sigh, Daphne scooped up a tiny gold mesh bag as she passed the bed and left the room.

She had no trouble spotting Adam as she stepped off the elevator. His bright golden hair shone like a beacon under the crystal chandeliers in the lobby. *My Greek god*, she thought, her heart full of tenderness as her eyes swept over him. Then she grinned. Impatient Greek god, she amended.

Adam stood by one of the rounded Doric columns near the hotel's impressive front desk, head bent as he studied the swirling pattern of the muted red and gold carpet. His stance was aggressive and his hands were again stuffed into the front pockets of his slacks, causing the material to stretch tautly over his firm backside. The set of his shoulders was rigid. She had seen him stand just exactly that way more times that she could remember, waiting for her. Punctuality had not been one of her virtues in the old days.

"Adam?" Daphne touched his shoulder as she came up behind him.

He whirled around as if she had poked him with a cattle prod, and Daphne took a quick half step backward to avoid being knocked over by the abruptness of his movement.

"Daphne," he began in the half-lecturing voice that she knew so well. He glanced at his watch as he spoke, and a quick frown creased his forehead. "You're on time," he said disbelievingly.

"Well, don't look so amazed." Daphne's husky voice was gently teasing. "It's not polite."

"Oh, it's not that," he denied quickly.

Daphne's arched eyebrows rose and her mouth quirked up at one corner.

"Okay, you're right. I'm amazed. Flabbergasted, actually." His admission came with a quick, engaging grin and he took her hand as he spoke, tucking it into the crook of his elbow as he turned her in the direction of the ballroom. Daphne's fingers curled automatically around the hard curve of his bicep. "It's just that I'd already resigned myself to the usual interminable wait."

"Interminable? Now really, Adam. Don't exaggerate. You never had to wait *that* long for me."

It was Adam's turn to lift a disbelieving eyebrow, his blond head cocked to one side as he smiled down at her.

"Well, okay, maybe once or twice." she admitted. "But that's all," she added as they neared the entrance to the ballroom.

As if by mutual consent, they paused just short of the open double doors and surveyed the scene before them. The dance floor was full to overflowing, music and laughter spilling across the threshold as smiling couples dipped and swayed to the Big Band sound of the orchestra. A huge mirrored ball twirled lazily overhead, sprinkling random rainbows of light over the revelers, while white-coated waiters worked the fringes of the floor, serving those who preferred to sit at the tiny white-draped tables instead of dance. It was a gay, inviting scene but neither of them made a move to join in.

"Yoo-hoo, Adam! Oh, A-a-a-dam," Sunny McCorkle called out as she danced past the door in the arms of her husband, Brian. One hand fluttered in the direction of the tables. "We're sitting over—" She broke off when she caught sight of Daphne. For just a second, she looked as guilty as a kid who'd been caught with her hand in the cookie jar, and then her face split with a self-satisfied, ear-to-ear grin. "Come join us after this dance," she said, giving them a thumbs-up sign before disappearing into the crowd again.

"I'm beginning to smell a rat," Adam said softly.

"Only just beginning?" Daphne glanced up at him through her thick lashes, eyes twinkling. "I smelled one hours ago."

Adam's blue eyes twinkled back. "And I don't think this particular rat should be allowed to get away with her little scheme, do you?"

"I think she aleady has," Daphne pointed out, a slight nod of her head indicating his hand covering hers where it lay on his arm.

"Well, then, she shouldn't be allowed to gloat over her success."

Daphne smiled. "What do you suggest we do to prevent that?"

Adam considered that for a moment. "Didn't someone mention a quiet drink somewhere? *Away* from all this noise and confusion?"

"Yes, I think someone did." Daphne glanced at the dance floor again and then back up at him. "It *is* awfully crowded in there, isn't it?"

"Hmm," Adam agreed as he steered her away from the door. "Be like trying to dance in a sardine can."

Together, they turned and silently, still arm in arm, crossed the wide lobby and entered a dimly lit cocktail lounge on the other side.

Adam guided Daphne to one of the tiny tables in the farthest corner of the room, silently signaling to the cocktail waitress who stood at one end of the bar. "I'll have a Chivas on the rocks," he said when she hurried over to take their order. "Daphne? Do you still drink rum and coke?"

Daphne shook her head, her long crystal earrings sparkling in the candlelight as she did so. "I'll have a Brandy Alexander, please."

She laid her mesh purse on the table, her eyes skimming over the dimly lit lounge as Adam repeated their order to the cocktail waitress. It was small and intimate with a gleaming mahogany bar and smoked, beveled mirrors. The bar stools were upholstered in burgundy leather and the small round cocktail tables were covered in deep-rose linen and decorated with fat pink candles in hurricane lamps. There was no room for a dance floor and no place for a band, but a baby grand sat on a raised platform at one end of the room. A woman in a long black dress was playing soft sad songs with a muted touch.

"This is nice," she said to Adam when the cocktail waitress had gone away. "Cozy and quiet."

"Think we'll be safe here?"

Daphne's forehead wrinkled in a frown. "Safe from what?"

"From one very lovely redheaded rat." Adam leaned an elbow on the table, cupping his chin in his hand, and grinned at her over the flickering candle flame. "She'll go crazy wondering where we've gone," he said with satisfaction.

Daphne laughed delightedly. "Oh, God, she will, won't she? Well, it serves her right! I swear, I could have *killed* her when I looked out into the audience tonight and saw..." Her voice trailed off as she caught his eye. "Oh, dear, that doesn't sound very gracious, does it? I just meant—" she waved one hand distractedly "—that, well, it was a surprise, that's all and..."

"Hey, it's okay. I understand. It was a complete surprise for me, too, you know. You could have knocked me over with a feather when I saw you walk out onto that stage." He fell silent as the cocktail waitress approached with their drinks, leaning back in his chair so that she could set them down on the tiny table. "Biggest damn surprise of my life," he continued when she had gone again. He picked up his drink.

"Well, here's to old times." He paused for just a heartbeat, his glance catching Daphne's over the rim of the glass. "And to new ones," he added softly. His eyes held hers, telling her exactly what he hoped those "new times" would involve. *I want you*, they said, more clearly, more eloquently, than mere words ever could.

Daphne sucked in her breath. There it was again, she thought. That change in him. That utterly devastating directness that was so... so utterly devastating! She wondered briefly how many women it had taken to make him so sure of himself—and hated every single one of them!

"To new ones," she said diffidently, feeling suddenly like a young girl on her very first date. She stared down into her glass for a moment, idly poking her plastic straw into the thick ice cream and brandy drink, calling herself six kinds of a fool for letting him rattle her so easily. All it had taken was a hot glance from those blue eyes and a veiled innuendo. No other man in eleven years had ever rattled her so.

But then, she thought wryly, no other man was Adam.

"So," she said then, determined to break the silence that held them. "Tell me what you've been doing for the past eleven years."

Adam eyed her for a brief moment, a considering look on his face, and then he lifted his broad shoulders in a shrug and let her lead him away from the topic that was on both their minds. "Studying," he said. "Working."

"Be more specific," Daphne ordered. She lifted her straw, licked the end of it, and laid it on the cocktail napkin beside her drink. "What did you do after you graduated from med school?"

"Took my state boards."

"And then?" she prodded, amused by the return to his usual laconism. Apparently, he hadn't changed as much as she'd first thought. Getting Adam to talk about himself had always been about as easy as getting blood from a stone.

"And then there were two years of rotating internship, three years of residency in general surgery, a year in orthopedics, and then, finally, another two years residency in plastic surgery," he said, summarizing eight years of hard work and sacrifice into one sentence.

"All at the same hospital in L.A.?"

"Yes, how did you know?"

Daphne smiled sweetly. "A little rat told me."

"Busy little rat, isn't she? What else did she tell you?" he said, reaching for his drink.

"Not much." Daphne shrugged and the neckline of her silk dress slid downward, revealing an equally silky shoulder. "Just that you had moved to L.A., is...all," she finished softly, caught by the look in Adam's eyes.

He was caught, too, his drink held halfway to his mouth, his eyes following the slide of her dress. Then he blinked, as if trying to free himself, and brought the glass to his lips. But he still watched her, his lambent gaze caressing her bare shoulder as he took a sip.

Daphne's breath seemed to catch somewhere in her throat. Her tongue snaked out, licking suddenly dry lips. "So." She fingered her sleeve, nudging it upward. "How long have you been back in San Francisco?"

"Almost six months now." His voice sounded hoarse, and he paused to clear it. "A position opened up here on the staff of Children's, Brian McCorkle recommended me and—" he smiled suddenly, lifting his glass as if to make another toast "—here I am, back in my old hometown."

"And loving it."

"Yes," he admitted, watching intently as she lifted her glass to her mouth. "There's no place quite like the City by the Bay."

"Hmm," Daphne agreed. Her tongue snaked out again, nervously licking a bit of ice cream from her lips. Adam's eyes followed the movement. "I've heard San Francisco's become a mecca for bachelors," she said then, trying for some sort of cool, some sort of distance, some sort of *anything* to diffuse the heat that was building in his eyes. "The, uh, handsome heterosexual types, that is. I understand they're at a real premium."

"So I've heard," he said, giving her his slow sleepy smile. She wondered if he knew he was doing it. Or if he knew what that smile did to her insides. They were quivering madly, like a soft tower of jello being shaken on a plate. And Adam was doing the shaking.

"Only heard? Aren't women chasing you all over the hospital?" Her tone, meant to be teasing, came out breathless and intimate instead. And inquiring, as if she had a burning interest in his answer. Or a right to know.

But Adam didn't answer her question. "Why don't we talk about you now?" he suggested. "What does it take to become a success as a fashion designer?"

"Work, work and more work." She strove to make her voice less breathy, more... casual. "In that order."

"Well, it has obviously paid off," he complimented her. "From what I saw tonight, it looks as if you've become a raging success—"

"Only fair to middlin'," Daphne interrupted, waggling her left hand in the air in a so-so gesture.

"Just like you always said you would," he finished. His long fingers idly twisted his glass in small circles on the rose-colored tablecloth. "You didn't stay with that department store very long."

"No," she answered, wondering how he had known that. Sunny, probably, she decided. "Those quilted jackets I was doing for Bloomie's were only a flash in the pan. In one season." She snapped her fingers. "Out the next."

"So what happened?"

"Oh, I got a job with a house and..." She paused as Adam began to smile. "Not *that* kind of house," she said, smiling back. Adam, despite his serious outlook on life, had always had a rather whimsical sense of humor. Daphne was glad to see that he hadn't lost it. "A *design* house. Anyway, I learned more there in one month than I had in the whole two years of fashion college. In less than a year my boss decided I was ready to do a few designs on my own—under the house name, of course. I did that for almost three years. And then—" she hesitated and then plunged ahead "—then Miles and I decided to go into business for ourselves and, well, the rest is history."

Adam's smile disappeared. "Miles," he said and flashed her a quick look that she couldn't quite read. "He was your husband."

"Yes," she said softly and then fell silent for a moment, gazing absently into her drink as if suddenly lost in thought. Her eyes grew a bit misty. "Poor Miles," she sighed, almost to herself.

"I'm sorry, I shouldn't have brought it up." Adam's voice was tight, as if it hurt him to say the words. "It upsets you to talk about it."

"No, I—" she began, and then stopped. It didn't upset her to talk about it, not the way Adam meant. It was just that she had never really loved Miles, not in the way she had loved—still loved—Adam. The thought always made her feel a little guilty, a little ashamed of herself and a little sorry for Miles because, as her husband, he should've had all the love she had to give. It was regret, not pain, that made her eyes grow misty. And sitting here with Adam, wanting him the way she did, only made that regret all the more poignant. Her only consolation was that Miles had probably never known that she had any more love to give and, so, was content with what little she offered.

"No, it doesn't upset me to talk about him. Really," she assured Adam. "It's been almost three years since the accident."

"How did it happen?" he asked quietly.

"Miles was driving up to a friend's place in Connecticut," she told him, her husky voice soft and even. "It was a Friday night, very late, and he was hit head-on by a drunk driver. The doctors assured me that he died almost instantly."

"Daphne, I'm sorry. Sorry, and terribly ashamed."

"Ashamed?" A slight frown wrinkled her smooth brow for a moment. "Why?"

"For that crack I made backstage. I had no right dismissing another man's death so . . . so callously. Even if—" his fingers showed white where they gripped his glass "—*especially* if it would give me something I wanted."

It took her a minute to comprehend what he was saying. Then it hit her. *"I should say I'm sorry, shouldn't I?"* he had said. *"But I'd be lying. I make it a rule never to make love to married women. And I've suddenly discovered that I want, very much, to make love to you."*

If he should be ashamed for saying it, then *she* should be ashamed for the thrill his words had given her. And she wasn't.

She reached across the table, covering his hand with hers. "Please, Adam, don't. I know you didn't mean it."

"Ah, but I did." His lips twisted in a self-deprecating smile. "Oh, not quite the way it sounded. I'm not really glad another man is dead." He reversed the position of their hands so that hers was lying under his and his thumb rubbed, ever so lightly, across the back of her wrist as he spoke. His eyes were lowered as he watched the movement. "But I am glad that he isn't standing between us."

"So am I," Daphne whispered. *Oh, so am I!*

He looked up at that, and his hand tightened on hers. She couldn't quite read the message in his eyes. Desire, of course. That had never been far from the surface between them. But there was something else there, too. Relief? Understanding? Need? Uncertainty? Yes, all those, she thought, but something else, too. Something she couldn't quite put her finger on.

He stood, pulling her to her feet. "Why don't we go have that dance now? It's time."

Yes, Daphne thought. *More than time.*

She picked up her purse and waited quietly, patiently, while Adam took out his wallet and dropped a couple of folded bills to the table. Then, silently, hand in hand, they walked back toward the ballroom.

Just as they reached the threshold, the orchestra began a slow, sweet number, and without a pause Adam swung her onto the crowded dance floor. His right hand settled on the small of her back, pulling her close to his body. His left hand reached for hers, intending to twine her fingers with his, but she held her purse in that hand.

"Here, let me take that," Adam said, his warm breath tickling the wispy curls at her temple as he spoke.

He took the tiny mesh purse from her fingers and slipped it into the pocket of his coat, then reached for her hand again. Their fingers linked, palms touching, and he brought her hand to his chest, turning her wrist slightly so that it was resting snugly against the black satin lapels of his jacket.

She moved more fully into Adam's embrace, settling into him without even thinking about it, her body seeming to know, to remember, the way they had always danced together. Her head nestled beneath his chin, her left hand unconsciously seeking the soft, short hairs at the nape of his neck. The movement caused the wide neckline of her dress to slide down again, baring the opposite shoulder, but Daphne didn't notice. She burrowed more deeply into him.

Sighing, his eyes closed, Adam lowered his head to rest his cheek against her hair. The back of his hand pressed against the top of her breast as they swayed to the slow, soft music.

Daphne's eyes closed, too, and her heart began to beat a little faster. She had to make a conscious effort to keep her breathing even. She needn't have bothered. Adam's breath was just as uneven, his heart was beating just as fast—and he was making no effort to hide it at all.

"See what you do to me," he said shakily, turning her hand between their bodies so that it lay flat against his chest. His heart thudded into her palm.

"Me, too," she whispered. She moved his hand, placing it over the curve of her silk-covered breast, letting him feel the rapid pounding of her own heart. He drew a sharp breath and his fingers curled for a moment, caressing her. Then his hand slid up to the slim column of her neck and he tilted her head back, the ball of his thumb under her chin. Her eyes were still closed, the better to savor his touch.

"Daphne." The word was a caress. A curse. A prayer. A question. "Daphne, look at me." His voice was low and taut, intense with emotion.

Daphne opened her eyes and gazed up at him. His eyes were blazing: a bright, burning, scorching blue. It was like looking into a raging inferno of long-suppressed desire. And, as she always had when faced with the fire in his eyes, Daphne melted.

"Yes," she said, answering his unspoken question. Her voice was little more than a sensuous purr.

Adam stopped dancing, oblivious to the couples who still swirled around them. "When?"

"Now." Daphne's eyes closed again and her head fell forward onto his chest. "Please."

Adam bent his head, touching his mouth, almost reverently, to the exposed curve of her shoulder. Then, clutching her hand in his, he led her from the ballroom.

4

THEY WERE STILL HOLDING HANDS when they stepped off the elevator on Daphne's floor. Their palms were pressed tightly, hotly together, their fingers intertwined like two frightened, lovesick teenagers who have finally, irrevocably decided to do something about their feelings for each other.

Only I wasn't this scared the first time, Daphne thought, taking two steps to every one of Adam's as they hurried down the long narrow corridor. *I wasn't this excited. And, oh God, I wasn't nearly this hungry!*

"Your key?" Adam said tersely as they came to an abrupt halt in front of the door to her hotel room.

"It's in your pocket," she answered, equally brief, her eyes focused on the curved brass numbers that adorned the door. She was afraid to look up at Adam, afraid to allow herself even one more glance into those burning blue eyes of his before they got into the privacy of her room. She was afraid that, if she did, she'd make a complete fool of herself by melting into a molten little heap of whimpering need right there on the pale gold carpet of the hallway.

Adam, apparently, was no better off. "Your key?" he repeated, as if he hadn't heard her. His voice was low, strained.

"It's in your pocket. You put my purse in . . ." Daphne began a trifle impatiently, glancing up as she spoke. The words caught in her throat. *I was right not to look at him*, she thought, unable to tear her eyes away now that she had.

Adam's expression was slightly dazed, his firm lips full and softer looking than they had been just a minute ago. He was staring at her mouth as if he could barely restrain himself from kissing her senseless.

Daphne's stomach began to quiver, the sensation rapidly moving outward and lower, causing little waves of need to radiate in all directions until even her knees were shaking. "You put my purse in your pocket," she repeated, barely managing to get the words out. "And the key...the key..." she faltered, licking suddenly dry lips with the tip of her tongue.

Adam gave a muffled groan and his hands came up to grip her shoulders. He lowered his head, blindly seeking her mouth with his.

"My purse, Adam," she whispered hoarsely, stopping him with a hand against his chest.

Adam groaned again, in protest this time, but he let her go and reached into his pocket, retrieving the tiny mesh bag. "Hurry," he pleaded, pressing it into her hand.

Silently, her fingers trembling, Daphne took it from him, extracted the key and unlocked the door. The room was in shadows, illuminated only by the narrow wedge of light peeking around the edge of the bathroom door. Before Daphne could even begin to grope along the wall for a light switch, Adam pushed her inside, slammed the door with a ferocious bang and hauled her into his arms.

"Oh, God, Daphne," she heard him say, just before his mouth found hers in the darkness, claiming it with a savage hunger. Her purse fell to the floor as she flung her arms around his neck. She stretched on tiptoe, her mouth answering his, her arms clinging to him like a drowning woman clutching a life preserver.

The thrust of his tongue was almost manic, seeking, searching, as their mouths twisted and turned upon each other. Her fingers threaded through the soft golden strands of his hair, holding his head as if she were afraid he might somehow disappear into thin air. But disappearing was the farthest thing from Adam's mind.

His hands roamed her back while he kissed her, kneading the curves of her spine and shoulders, sizzling over apricot silk as he sought a way to the warm soft skin beneath the dress.

Daphne, too, began seeking bare flesh. Her hands dropped to his neck, whispering over the skin of his nape, and slid under the collar of his evening jacket. With her mouth still sealed tightly to his, she managed to ease the jacket off his shoulders, momentarily forcing him to release his hold on her as she pushed it down his arms. It dropped, unheeded, to the carpeted floor.

Her arms circled his waist then, as his went back around her, and her hands tugged impatiently at the fabric of his shirt until it came free of his slacks. With a muffled cry, she pressed her palms flat against the smooth bare skin of his lower back, pulling him even more tightly to her.

Obligingly, Adam arched, thrusting his hips forward as he instinctively sought the soft cradle of her thighs. But their heights were too disparate, despite her high-heels, for either of them to feel the pressure where they most wanted it. Adam bent his knee, insinuating it between her parted thighs, and slid his hands down to cup her buttocks, lifting her into his aroused body.

Daphne whimpered softly, deep in her throat, and began to move against him. Her hands flexed rhythmically against the bare flesh of his back, her thighs tight against the welcome intrusion of his.

Adam's tongue thrust deeper into her open mouth, blatantly imitating the more subtle movements of his hips. His hands feathered over her pliant body, frantic now as he looked for a way to get her out of the dress without letting her go. He managed to loosen the belt enough so that it slid to the floor, but that was as far as he could go. His skillful, seeking fingers found neither buttons nor zipper.

He lifted his head, breathing in great, ragged gulps of air. "Wait," he gasped, trying to stop Daphne's hands as she fumbled with the fastening of his cummerbund.

But Daphne didn't seem to hear him. Her fingers continued to struggle under his and the pleated cummerbund fell away. He caught her hands in his as she reached for the zipper of his slacks.

"Daffy, wait," he ordered gruffly, fighting the urge to simply tear the dress from her body.

Daphne stilled, the urgency of his command getting through to her. Her head tilted back as she looked up at him. She was breathing deeply, a bit raggedly, her breasts resting against his heaving chest. She blinked, trying to focus. "Why?"

"Because I don't know how to get this damn dress off you without tearing it, that's why."

"Damn dress?" She straightened away from him a little and peered down at herself in the darkness, past the two pairs of hands that were still pressed firmly against the waistband of his slacks. "It's a very nice dress," she said inanely, a faint hint of indignation in her tone.

"Very nice," he agreed, sudden reluctant laughter rumbling deep in his chest. "Except that there aren't any buttons or zippers on it. How do I get it off you?"

In answer, Daphne withdrew her hands from under his and, in two quick movements, unfastened the small crystal buttons on either wrist. Then, crossing her arms in front of her body, she grasped the elastic waistline, pulled the dress up over her head and dropped four-hundred dollars worth of pure silk inside out on the carpeted floor.

"There," she said matter-of-factly. "It's off." She stood before him wearing only a pair of expensive high-heeled shoes, very sheer French panty hose and a strapless bra made of some pale shimmery material the color of heavily creamed coffee. Her breasts rose softly above the satin bra, their upper slopes lightly sprinkled with pale golden-brown freckles that seemed to dance and shimmer with each quick breath she drew.

Adam gulped audibly, his sudden laughter stilled as quickly as it had come, and reached for her again.

But Daphne stepped back, shaking her head, her crystal earrings brushing softly against her neck with the movement. At the same time she reached out, grasped the end of his bow tie with trembling fingers and tugged it loose. It came undone easily and she drew it out from under the collar of his shirt, tossing it to the floor with one hand, reaching for the topmost button on his shirt with the other.

Adam put his hands on her waist then, over the lace band of her panty hose, as if to steady her. His long hard fingers curved around to the small of her back. His thumbs rested against her hipbones, rotating slowly.

Daphne gasped softly but continued with her task. Head bent, intent on what she was doing, she unbuttoned the first button... the second... the third, her fingers becoming a bit more frantic and hurried as each one revealed a bit more of Adam's hard golden chest. At last it was done and she slipped her hands under the shirt, laying her palms ever so gently over the hard curve of his lower pectorals.

Adam sucked in his breath, his chest going very still beneath her caressing hands, but she could feel his heart slamming into her palm. Twice as hard, twice as fast as it had been downstairs in the ballroom.

So soft, she thought. *So warm. So exactly as her hands remembered him!*

She straightened her fingers, threading them up through the tangle of silky hair on his chest and then down again, until she could feel one hard male nipple against the center of each sensitive palm. She sighed deeply, raggedly, eyes closed as she savored the feel of the man she had thought she would never, ever touch again.

Adam's hands slid up her back as she stood there with her hands on his chest, and deftly released the clasp of her bra. Daphne's eyes fluttered open, bright as liquid gold as she stared up into the blue furnace of his. She lifted her arms from her sides, letting the bra fall away from her body. Her breasts were full and firm and aching, the nipples pale cocoa-brown and hard as little pebbles, puckered tightly with desire. She moved forward until her breasts were touching his chest, until the little golden whorls of hair were tickling her sensitive skin.

So exactly as she remembered him, she thought, stifling the excited little moan that rose to her lips.

Adam crushed her to him, his mouth taking hers in a quick hard kiss that seemed designed to brand her lips with his passion and possession. Then he lifted her in his arms and carried her across the gold carpet to the bed.

Daphne retained just enough presence of mind to kick her shoes off along the way. They hit the carpeted floor with soft little thumps that neither of them noticed. Then Adam laid her gently on the turned-down bed and straightened up to remove the rest of his clothes. Lying there, watching him peel down to bare skin, Daphne ceased to have any mind at all.

She half sat up, intending to shimmy out of her panty hose, but Adam bent over her, gloriously naked now, and pressed her back into the pale green sheets. Hooking trembling hands in the waistband of her one remaining garment, he drew them past her hips and down her legs. Standing there beside the bed, her panty hose dangling inside out from one hand, he gazed down at her.

His eyes traveled slowly up over her body, making a visual feast of her ankles and calves and smooth creamy thighs, leaving ripples of sensation fluttering across the softly rounded belly, and the full, taut breasts that rose and fell with each quick breath.

Daphne, lying so still under his heated gaze, was making a survey of her own. Her eyes, gleaming golden in the dim room, traveled greedily over his body, taking inventory, remembering...

His legs and arms were still corded with the long, lean muscles of a regular runner, still dusted with that sprinkling of soft blond hair that gave him the look of a gilded *David*. His shoulders were still those of a football player. His chest was still deep and broad, the flat male nipples looking like tiny bronze disks nestled among the silky chest hairs. Avidly, her eyes starved for the sight of him, she followed the narrowing arrow of chest hair down the flat-muscled wall of his stomach to where it widened again. He was full and hard and straining eagerly toward her.

Her eyes skittered back to his face and found his eyes waiting for her. They stared at each other, glittering golden eyes burning into blazing blue ones, for a full thirty seconds without saying a word.

"You're so damn beautiful," he said finally, his deep voice betraying none of the trembling that had taken control of his body.

"So are you." Daphne lifted her arms from the bed, opening her body to his. "Now," she whispered huskily, repeating the words she had said to him while they danced. "Please."

He came to her in one swift movement, thrusting forward into her waiting, willing moistness. Her body arched off the bed as he entered her, both of them moaning in satisfaction as he buried himself deep inside her. He pressed his hips down and forward, trying to hold her still as he fought for the control that her eagerness and passion had taken from him. But Daphne continued to move, her legs coming up to wrap around his waist, her hips bucking rhythmically under his.

"Daphne." His voice was ragged, breathless. "Oh, God, baby, slow down. I..." His hands slid down her torso to her hips, holding her. "I'll be too fast for you if you don't slow down."

"No." She panted the words into his neck. "No, you won't...not this time...not now." She pressed her nails into the hard curve of his buttocks. "Oh, Adam, *please*," she urged frantically.

Assured that he wasn't going to leave her wanting, Adam slipped his hands under her hips, fitting her body even more closely to his, and began to move. His hips pumped rhythmically, strongly, against hers. One minute...two, and then Daphne's body stiffened like an overstrung bow and she let loose a low moan of ecstatic pleasure that was echoed a moment later by a deep cry from Adam.

It took several long minutes for their breathing to slow to rhythms that even approached normal and several more after that before Adam reluctantly raised his head from the warm sweet space between her neck and shoulder. He stared down into her eyes for a brief second and the look that passed between them was somehow hesitant, almost shy, as if neither of them knew quite what to say now that the storm of passion had passed.

Well, Daphne thought, *what do you say to an ex-husband when you find yourself in bed with him after a separation of eleven years?*

Before she could come up with a suitable answer, Adam lifted himself from her body and rolled over onto his back. He lay beside her, silent and still, not touching, as if waiting for her to speak first.

Daphne shivered, feeling suddenly cold and almost—almost, but not quite—ashamed of her display of unleashed passion. She had gone to bed with Adam tonight because, despite everything, she loved him. And she believed, wholeheartedly, that that love was nothing to be ashamed of.

But why had Adam gone to bed with her?

His motives hadn't seemed important *before* the act. Only her need had been important then. But now, *after* that fierce terrible need had been assuaged and she was lying there beside him feeling absurdly lost and alone, knowing his motives seemed like the most important thing in the world.

She dismissed love—his love—as a contributing factor. She was wise enough to know that it wasn't love that had driven Adam to her bed tonight. He had, after all, been the one to file for divorce all those years ago. Lust, then, she decided. Adam had always been a very physical man, and she'd always been able to arouse him with little more than a look. Lust and, as a recent article in *Cosmopolitan* had suggested, propinquity, nostalgia and a certain morbid curiosity about what it would be like to have sex with an ex-spouse. On her part, as well as his, she acknowledged, forcing herself to face the plain unvarnished truth.

Because she *had* wondered, especially during the calm placid years with Miles, if the explosive passion Adam had kindled in her was only a memory that had been exaggerated by time and distance. Well, she didn't have to wonder anymore. No mere memory could make her feel the way Adam had tonight.

Daphne turned her head and found him staring at her in the darkness. His eyes seemed to reflect every bit of the confusion she felt, but in the dim light, she couldn't be sure. His hand moved between them on the bed, his little finger curling around hers.

"Daphne, I—" he began.

His words were cut off by a series of sharp staccato beeps. They both jumped as if a whip had been cracked over their nude bodies and then Adam jackknifed to his feet. "Damn beeper!" He took three long steps across the room and scooped his tuxedo jacket up off the floor. Hurriedly, he rummaged through the pockets, found the small rectangular metal box and shut it off.

"I'm sorry." He gestured at the beeper in his hand, his expression registering something that looked suspiciously like relief. Daphne recognized it because she felt it, too. He had been about to say something about the situation they were in, about to utter some banal commonplace to smooth it over or, worse, offer an apology. Daphne didn't want to hear it, and she was glad the beeper had stopped him from saying it.

"Probably the hospital," he said then, crossing the room to sit down on the edge of the rumpled bed with his back to her. He switched on the squat bedside lamp and reached for the phone. "I have to call my service," he mumbled, glancing over his shoulder at her as he dialed. "Could be an emergency."

Daphne nodded and scurried under the covers when he turned back to answer the voice on the other end of the line. She sat with her knees pulled to her chest, the covers held under her chin with both hands, and listened to his side of the phone conversation.

"Umm-hmm. When?" he said into the phone. His voice was cool, professional. The unflappable Dr. Forrest, Daphne thought wryly. She wondered what the person on the other end of the telephone would say if they could see him sitting there naked, feeling around on the floor for his clothes.

"How long has she been complaining of the pain?" He found his white jockey shorts and, phone wedged between his ear and shoulder, used both hands to pull them on. "Umm-hmm. No, I realize she can be difficult to deal with, and I left specific instructions to call me if— No, it's all right, really, you didn't interrupt anything important." He maneuvered his slacks over his feet and up to his thighs. "Yes, fine. Fifteen minutes." He dropped the receiver into the cradle and stood, zipping up his slacks as he did so.

"That was the hospital," he said unnecessarily, looking around for his shirt. He found it lying half under the bedside table. He picked it up, shoved his arms into the sleeves and began fastening the buttons. "One of my patients seems to be experiencing some unusual pain after an abdominal tuck. I don't think it's anything really serious, but I don't want to take any chances." He sat down again to put on his shoes and socks. "I hope you understand."

"Yes, of course. I understand," she said, understanding only that he couldn't get out of the room fast enough.

Dressed now, his cummerbund and bow tie stuffed into a jacket pocket, Adam leaned across the width of the bed and touched Daphne's shoulder through the blankets. She forced herself not to jerk away from him. "I'm sorry about this, Daffy. About leaving you like this right after..." He hesitated slightly, not knowing what to say.

Daphne stopped him before he could go any further. "It's okay," she said woodenly, still hearing those words he had said to the nurse, or whoever it was on the other end of the phone. *You didn't interrupt anything important.* "I really do understand. Duty calls."

Adam straightened, his expression disconcerted and doubtful, but Daphne wasn't looking at him. She was studying the polish on her left thumbnail. "Maybe we could get together for lunch tomorrow," he suggested. Rather halfheartedly, Daphne thought. An obvious sop to his conscience.

Daphne didn't want any part of any "mercy lunches." *You didn't interrupt anything important.* "I don't think so," she stated.

"But—"

"No, really, I can't." She lifted her head, forcing herself to smile at him. "I have to catch an early plane home tomorrow." She slid from the bed, wrapping the bedspread around her as she rose. "So you see, it's really kind of fortunate that that call came when it did." She rounded the end of the bed and headed for the door of her room, the green and gold spread trailing behind her like a train. "I need to get up awfully early tomorrow." She gave him what she hoped was a casual look as she reached for the doorknob. "And I'm a real grouch when I don't get enough sleep. Remember?" She pulled open the door, shielding her half-clad body behind it. "Well, it's been lovely seeing you again, Adam," she went on, tacitly inviting him to leave. "We must do it again sometime."

Adam hesitated for a moment, irresolute, unsure how to respond. Something flickered in his eyes for a moment, and then he shrugged and forced a smile. Tossing his tuxedo jacket over his shoulder, he strolled toward Daphne. He stopped at the open door and lifted her chin with his free hand. Daphne clutched the bedspread tighter.

"Give me a call next time you're in town and we will," he suggested, dropping a quick, careless kiss on her astonished mouth before he left.

5

"DAPHNE, TELEPHONE!" Elaine shouted to make herself heard across the length of the busy workroom. "Line two," she added, carelessly dropping the receiver back onto the cradle of the phone as she punched the hold button.

Daphne looked up from her drawing board, her stomach clenching in anticipation. "Who is it?"

"Clare." Elaine made a face as she got up from her desk. "From the Dragon Lady Boutique. *Again*."

Daphne's stomach unclenched. She placed the violet pencil she had been using in the shallow trough at the bottom of her slanted drawing table. Pushing up the drooping sleeves of her camel-colored silk knit sweater with a resigned gesture, she reached for the ivory wall phone that hung to the left of her cluttered work space.

"She says we positively, absolutely did not include the beaded belts with that last shipment of dresses," Elaine began to explain before Daphne had a chance to lift the receiver. "I *told* her they were packed separately so as not to snag the dresses, but does she listen to me? No-o-o, of course not. She wants to talk to you. I *told* her you were too busy but—"

Daphne shook her head at her assistant, silencing her tirade, and put the receiver to her ear. "Clare, how nice to hear from you," she said, lying through her teeth as she proceeded to verbally pour liberal amounts of oil—or something—over troubled waters.

Strictly speaking, this sort of thing was Elaine's job, Daphne thought with a flash of irritation as she listened to the complaining voice on the other end of the phone. Elaine was supposed to handle orders and back orders, invoices and bills, shipments and slipups; and she had her own perky little eighteen-year-old secretary to help her.

So why, thought Daphne, *am I talking to the Dragon Lady? As if I didn't have enough to do!*

She was up to her ears in the final designs for next fall's collection, up to her ears in plans for an upcoming charity benefit, up to her ears in New York's slushy lionlike March weather, up to her ears period!

"Damn it, Elaine!" She began chastising the young woman as soon as she hung up. "I can't be interrupted every ten minutes with a call that you could have handled perfectly well by yourself. What's the matter with you lat—" She stopped abruptly, suddenly realizing that every head in the room had snapped to attention at the sound of her voice.

There was a tiny millisecond of silence, nervous glances were exchanged as everyone reassured themselves that they were not her intended target, a few wry, long-suffering smiles were traded, a few shoulders raised in a "who knows?" sort of shrug. And then heads bent back over worktables, or lengths of fabric draped on long elegant bodies, and the hum of voices resumed as if nothing had happened. Except that Daphne realized she had nearly been shouting—again.

With a sigh, she propped both elbows on the drawing board and dropped her forehead into her cupped hands. "Damn," she swore softly.

She seemed to have been doing a lot of shouting in the past week. The volatile temper she had learned to control so well, losing it only when it would do her some good, seemed to be going off every twenty minutes. And it took embarrassingly little to light the fuse: models who were three minutes late for a fitting; the delivery boy from the deli downstairs bringing her tuna salad on white instead of wheat; Federal Express stopping by for a pickup five minutes later than they said they would; someone asking a simple question; the telephone. Especially the telephone. She kept hoping—and dreading—that it was Adam.

It was all *his* fault, damn him, she thought savagely. Good manners, if nothing else, should have prompted him to call by now. It wasn't as if she was expecting declarations of love, or even an invitation to dinner the next time she was in town, but he could at least have called to make sure she had got back to New York all right. That would have been the gentlemanly thing to do. And even if he didn't want to talk to her, he could have written a polite little note saying that he had enjoyed seeing her again, couldn't he? He could have sent her flowers. Something! Anything! This deafening silence from the West Coast was making her feel like a one-night stand. Which was probably just how he thought of her.

You didn't interrupt anything important. A man could hardly get any clearer than that!

Oh, well, chalk one up to experience, she told herself consolingly. Blame it on human nature and the law of averages. Because, according to all the current "experts," having a fling with one's ex-husband was almost boringly predictable; for some probably deep-seated masochistic reason, women seemed to do it all the time.

"Damn!" she said again, more forcefully this time.

"Daphne?" Elaine's voice was hesitant. "Look, I'm sorry, okay? I should have handled the Dragon Lady myself. I—"

"It's not your fault," Daphne said from behind her hands. "I shouldn't have yelled at you."

Elaine reached out, putting a tentative hand on Daphne's shoulder. "Hey, are you all right, boss?"

Daphne sighed and lifted her head. "I'm fine," she said, a smile of apology on her lips. She reached up and patted the hand on her shoulder. "Just fine, really," she added, and then grimaced. "Except for the fact that I've been acting like a raging bitch, that is. I'm sorry for coming on like the Red Queen." She gave Elaine's hand a light, affectionate squeeze before she released it. "Forgive me?" she said, reaching for the violet drawing pencil as she spoke.

"Oh, don't worry about it. I understand completely." Elaine shook her head, setting the glossy brown hair to bobbing around her chin. "*Men.*"

Daphne was amused in spite of herself. Elaine thought that men, individually or as a group, were the root of every woman's problems. "What makes you think it's a man? Haven't you ever heard of premenstrual tension? The rising incidence of stress among working women?"

"Oh, come on, Daphne. Be serious. You've never succumbed to premenstrual tension in your life. At least," she amended, "not since I've known you. And you love this business, stress and all. Besides—"

"Maybe I'm just hungry," Daphne suggested. "You know how cranky I get when I'm hungry."

Elaine shook her head, dismissing that argument. "Besides," she said again, hooking a sheaf of hair behind her ear with the tip of one finger. "I'm not blind, you know. I saw that big juicy kiss he planted on you backstage." Apparently, Elaine felt no need to further identify the "he" in question.

"Who?" Daphne tried, knowing it wouldn't work.

Elaine gave her a disgusted look.

"Okay, so he kissed me." Daphne sighed in mock resignation. "Big deal. One little kiss. A simple greeting between old—" she paused briefly, twisting the violet pencil between her fingers as she sifted through her mind for an appropriate word "—friends. But, contrary to what you're obviously thinking, that kiss has nothing to do with my, uh, my bad temper lately. That probably *is* just due to premenstrual tension. I do occasionally suffer from it, you know. Just like a normal woman."

"Uh-huh," Elaine grunted inelegantly. "Maybe. Except that I also saw you leave the ballroom together." She paused significantly. "The *second* time."

"Really?" Daphne's eyes narrowed in a not-so-subtle hint to drop the subject.

Elaine paid no heed. "Yes, really! And it didn't take a genius to see what the two of you were up to, either. It was as obvious as the nose on your face that—"

Daphne interrupted her before she could say another word. "What do you think of this new design?" she said very casually, gesturing toward the drawing on her worktable.

"Great." Elaine's praise was automatic; she didn't even glance down at the sketches and, oblivious to the hint that had become a full-fledged warning, she plunged recklessly ahead. "Personally, I think it's always a mistake to—"

Daphne interrupted her again. "Elaine, dear," she said patiently, pleasantly, her husky voice as quietly deadly as a knife blade. "You like your job, don't you?"

Elaine, finally recognizing the tone, not to mention the look in her employer's eyes, merely nodded.

"Well, then, what do you think of this new design?" She tapped twice on the drawing with the tip of one mocha-colored fingernail.

"It's, uh, great," Elaine said, and then looked down at the drawing for the first time.

Sketched in violet were two views, front and back, of an utterly simple, scandalously sexy little camisole and tap pants set. The camisole had tiny spaghetti straps holding up a low V-neck. The matching tap pants were bias cut with a lettuce-edge hem that gave them a fluttery, feminine look without detracting from the simple lines.

"Hey, it really *is* great," Elaine said again after ten seconds careful study. She slanted a quick look at her employer. "When did you decide to branch out into lingerie?"

Daphne shrugged. "A couple of days ago, I guess. All those evening clothes were beginning to look the same to me so I started doodling around with a few new ideas and came up with this. You know how it goes." She lifted the top drawing, laying it aside to reveal other sketches of her proposed line of lingerie. There were sexy little teddies cut high on the leg, utterly simple silk chemises with a bit of delicate embroidery on the bodice, slinky bias cut nightgowns with softly draped fronts and thigh-high side slits, short mantailored nightshirts and figure-flattering wrap-front robes. They were all done in her own signature style: completely feminine and totally sexy without relying on the excessive use of ruffles and lace.

"I thought I'd do everything in two color families," she told Elaine, her voice tinged with the excitement she always felt about new designs. "Violet, lilac and a pale silvery gray for the cool colors. Bronze, peach and a creamy ivory for the warm spectrum. All solids so that they can be mixed and matched within their color families. And everything in silk or silk blends. I definitely want to use a silk jacquard for some of the camisole and pant sets. Maybe some of the chemises, too. And, I think, a really rich panne velvet in the two darkest colors for the robes since it'll be for the fall season." She looked up at Elaine. "What do you think?"

"I think you've been doing more than just 'doodling around with a few new ideas.' These are really great, Daphne." Elaine picked up a couple of sketches to study them more closely. "They'll give a whole new meaning to the name Night Lights, won't they?"

Daphne grinned. "That's the idea."

"A whole new line, then, huh?" Elaine said, beginning to get excited about the possibilities herself. "Added to our regular evening clothes."

"Maybe." Daphne had learned to be a tiny bit more cautious over the years. "We'll see how this first collection goes over before we make any long-range plans for expansion."

"Oh, it'll be just wonderful!" Elaine stated emphatically. "Elegant, feminine, sexy. The collection has Daphne Granger written all over it!"

"Yes, but will it sell?"

"How can you ask that? I can hardly wait to have one of everything in the violet and lilac myself."

"Maybe so," Daphne teased, "but you're not exactly a paying cust—"

"Mrs. Granger, you have a call on line one," Elaine's eighteen-year-old assistant interrupted diffidently.

Daphne's head snapped up at the words, a half panicked, half inquiring look skittering over her face.

"It's Mrs. McCorkle," the girl added.

The panic receded instantly, replaced by righteous indignation. *Ah-ha*, Daphne thought, practically pouncing on the phone in her eagerness to express the feelings that had been bottled up for the past week. And who better to express them to than the very person—the rat—who was responsible for the emotional turmoil she found herself in.

"Sunny, you traitor!" Daphne said without preamble. "I ought to strangle you! If you were here right now I *would* strangle you. That was the lowest—"

"It's nice to hear from you, too," Sunny said cheerfully.

"The lowest, sneakiest trick you've ever pulled," Daphne accused. "You're responsible for this... this mess. You engineered the whole thing. I know you did!"

"Engineered what mess?"

"Don't give me that Miss Innocence routine. I know you, remember? You *knew* Adam was at Children's Hospital. You *knew* he was going to be at that charity benefit. Why didn't you tell me?"

"Oh, is *that* what this is all about?" Sunny's voice was innocence itself. Daphne could practically see her waving one hand in an airily dismissive gesture, her inch-long nails gleaming blood red—or whatever the color of the week was—as she did so. "I didn't think you were interested in what Adam was doing these days." She paused for just a beat. "Or are you?" she inquired silkily.

"No, I'm not," Daphne lied. "But I would have at least liked to have been warned that he was going to be there, you know."

"Why? I mean, if you don't care about him, what difference does it make?"

"Well, it was a bit of a shock, that's all." Daphne glanced sideways, realizing that Elaine was still standing next to her worktable, eyes wide as she blatantly listened to every word. She lowered her voice and turned more toward the wall. "I didn't expect to see him and it, uh, threw me off balance. A little," she amended quickly.

"In a pig's eye," Elaine mumbled from behind her.

Daphne hunched her shoulder, pointedly ignoring her assistant's commentary.

"Well, gee-whiz," Sunny was saying. "If I'd had any idea that just *seeing* him again was going to upset you this much I would have said something."

"I am not upset!"

"Well, you seemed to be getting along just fine when I saw you standing in the doorway to the ballroom. Quite chummy, actually. I remember telling Brian how friendly you two looked and—Hey," she interrupted herself, "where did you two disappear to anyway?"

"We went to the cocktail lounge for a drink." Daphne cast a quick look over her shoulder to see if Elaine was still standing by the drawing board. She was. "Don't you have anything better to do?" Daphne said irritably. "No, not you, Sunny. I was talking to Elaine." She pinned her assistant with a look. "Well?"

"Okay, okay. I'm going." Elaine moved a few feet away, one of Daphne's sketches still clasped in her hands. She lifted it to the light as if to examine it. "I'm gone."

Daphne turned back toward the wall.

"And, well, Brian and I wondered where you'd got to." Sunny was rattling on in her usual cheerful manner unaware, or unconcerned, that Daphne hadn't been listening to her. "Brian was right, as usual. He said you'd probably gone off by yourselves to catch up on old times."

"We didn't go off by ourselves," Daphne said, when Sunny finally paused for breath. "We went to the cocktail lounge."

"Whatever," Sunny agreed absently. "So, listen—as Brian is always reminding me, this is long distance—the reason I called is to invite you to a party next week. Now before you say no, Daphne," she hurried on before Daphne could say anything, "remember that you did tell me you'd be back in town then. That meeting with what's-her-name over at I. Magnin. And as long as you're going to be here anyway I thought, well, hell, why not come to our party? It'll be a real hoot! All the old gang's coming. Kathy and John Martinelli. Remember them? Still married and still fighting like cats and dogs," Sunny informed her gleefully. "Pippa Eaton, too.

Only I think it's Pippa Gerard now. Or is it Germain? She's married so many times that I can't keep track. And Gail Scott. And Carl Ferguson. Remember him? The one with the—"

"And Adam, too, I suppose?" Daphne interrupted.

"Well, of course, Adam, too! It's his party."

"I thought it was your party."

"Well, I'm *giving* it," Sunny said patiently, as if explaining something to a particularly backward child. "But it's *for* Adam. His thirty-seventh birthday, remember? It's sort of a welcome home, too, of course. We're all glad to see him back in San Francisco where he belongs. Brian thought—"

"You mean you're giving Adam a birthday party? And you expect me to come to it?" Daphne could hardly believe her ears.

"Well, yes. That's exactly what I expect." Sunny paused and a huge sigh wound its way through the telephone wires. "I mean, all the old gang's going to be there and you're part of the old gang," she continued, sounding like a small hurt child on the verge of tears. "You wouldn't want to spoil my party, would you?" she asked tremulously.

"I hardly think my not coming is going to spoil your party," Daphne said dryly, knowing quite well that Sunny was doing her level best to manipulate her into going.

"It will!" Sunny insisted. Daphne could almost see her bottom lip stuck out in a pout. "I've already told everyone that you'll be there. And they're all looking forward to seeing you again."

"Well, I'm sorry but you're just going to have to un-tell them because I'll be too busy to come."

"Oh, come on, Daphne, don't say a definite 'no,' okay? I know you're terribly busy and everything, and this trip to San Francisco is supposed to be business, but it would be so much fun if you could make it. Say you'll at least try to make it, okay? Please?" she wheedled. "Just *try* to stop by?"

Daphne, realizing that she had been manipulated by a master, said she'd try. "But don't count on it," she warned, knowing it would do no good.

"Terrific!" Sunny squealed, taking Daphne's partial concession as a total capitulation. "See you on the twenty-eighth. And wear something drop-dead sexy," she ordered, hanging up before Daphne could remind her that she'd only said she'd *try* to make it, not that she'd actually be there.

She reached out to put the phone back in its cradle, shaking her head as she did so. *That Sunny*, she thought, *give her an inch and she'll run away with it.*

Well, despite what she'd said to Sunny, she had no intention of going to Adam's birthday party. Why ask for trouble? Because that's what it would be, she told herself, trouble. That night with Adam had been a mistake. But with him right there in the flesh, looking at her with that burning heat in his eyes, she hadn't really cared.

Well, now she cared. Because now it hurt. And now she missed him as sharply, as deeply, as she had eleven years ago. For the past week, she had been weaving crazy, impossible dreams about happily-ever-afters that had ceased to be possible the day he filed for divorce.

No, she told herself, firmly pushing away the thought of seeing him again. *No, I'm not going to that party.*

"I think you should go." Elaine's words, so in tune with what she had just been thinking, made Daphne start with surprise.

She turned to look over her shoulder, the surprise fading as she realized that Elaine was only responding to the conversation she had overheard and not answsering Daphne's unspoken comment. "Oh, you do, do you?" she said, a warning light in her big golden-brown eyes.

"Yes, I do," Elaine stated emphatically. She put Daphne's sketch on the drawing board and wiped her hands nervously down the front of her neon-green miniskirt. "And if you'll promise not to bite my head off, I'll tell you why I think you should."

"I have a feeling I'm not going to like this," Daphne said, her voice resigned. "But go ahead, anyway." She cocked her head invitingly, her forearm resting against the edge of the drawing board. "Why do you think I should go to this party?"

"Because..." Elaine wiped her hands on her skirt again, pausing at the look in Daphne's eyes, and then rushed ahead. "Because, ever since he kissed you," she said, once again not bothering to define who "he" was, "you've been moping around like some lovesick teenager with a crush on the quarterback, that's why."

Daphne snapped upright. "Some lovesick teen—" she began indignantly, then stopped, knowing all too well how true the accusation was.

"Yes, a lovesick teenager," Elaine went on as if Daphne hadn't opened her mouth. "You practically jump out of your skin every time the phone rings. You're irritable and cranky. You snap at people for no reason." Elaine fixed her with an accusing stare when Daphne opened her mouth to refute it. "Don't try to deny it, Daphne. You know you have."

"I wasn't going to deny it," Daphne pointed out calmly.

"You weren't?" Elaine looked skeptical, and totally surprised that Daphne hadn't bitten her head off.

"I know I haven't been a joy to be around lately," she admitted with a small smile of self-deprecation. "But what I *don't* know is how you think my going to Adam's little birthday party is going to change things. The way I see it, it will only make it worse." She sighed and shook her head, firmly pushing the idea away. "No, the best thing for me to do is stay as far away from Adam as possible. I'll get over it, just like I did the last time," she murmured, lying to herself as well as Elaine.

"Oh, no, that's the worst thing you could do."

Daphne raised her eyebrows in silent query.

"No, really, it is. Just think about it a minute," Elaine urged. "If you stay away from him you'll think about him all the more. You'll wonder what it would be like if you got back together again and you'll remember how it was when you *were* together. Only you'll remember it better than it really was. Then you'll start to miss him so bad that you ache inside and you'll begin to dream about all the good times you had and forget all the bad ones. And there must have been some bad times," she pointed out reasonably, "or your marriage wouldn't have ended the way it did."

Daphne's mouth dropped open slightly as Elaine described her feelings to a T. Every word the younger woman said made perfect sense. It was exactly, *exactly*, what Daphne had been thinking and feeling for the past week.

"But," Elaine continued, warming to the subject, "if you go out to California, see him again, even have an affair, maybe... Well—" she shrugged philosophically "—it'll give you a chance to get him out of your system. See? And you'll probably realize that your relationship wasn't as good as you remembered."

"My God, Elaine," Daphne said, awed at her uncannily accurate reading of the situation. "How do you know so much?"

"Well, Suzie told me what you'd told her," she admitted reluctantly, misunderstanding Daphne's question. "About how you got married so young and the divorce and everything."

"No, I didn't mean that," Daphne murmured absently, too bemused by the good sense of what Elaine had said to be bothered by the fact that her friends had been gossiping about her. "I meant how did you know..." Her voice trailed off and she stared at Elaine for a moment without seeing her, her golden-brown eyes focused inward.

"How did I know what?" Elaine prodded.

"What? Oh, nothing. It wasn't important." She shook her head as if to clear it, and then smiled. "Do you think you could stand taking care of my cats for a couple of days?" she asked.

"You're going, then?"

"Yes," Daphne said decisively. "Yes, I'm going."

6

DAPHNE'S RESOLVE wasn't quite so firm as she sat in her rented LeBaron, trying to work up the nerve to get out from behind the wheel and go on into the party.

It looked like a fairly big party, she thought, eyeing the cars that lined both sides of the steep street for half a block in either direction. And it appeared to be in full swing.

The McCorkle house was brightly lit, a beacon in the thin, wispy fog that curled in from the bay. Light spilled through the fanciful stained-glass window above the door, casting oblongs of color across the wide brick steps and the multi-leveled redwood decking and potted shrubs that took the place of a front yard. Strategically placed spotlights highlighted the slanted roofs and sharp angles of the house, while a starkly modern street lamp cast its soft welcoming glow in a golden pool at the foot of the stairs. The muted throb of sixties rock music drifted out through the night air, punctuated now and again by sharp bursts of laughter, beckoning her to come join the fun.

And still Daphne sat in the car, her stomach fluttering worse than it did before a fashion show.

Oh, come on, she scolded herself. *Just get out and go in. There's nothing to be afraid of. Be brave*, she told herself, her fingers fussing with the red satin ribbon on Adam's birthday gift.

She had finally, after much thought, decided on a one-pound box of gourmet chocolate chunk cookies; soft and chewy and rich with Hawaiian macadamia nuts. They were homey without being homemade, extravagant without being expensive, impersonal without being uncaring, friendly without being intimate. And they said absolutely nothing about how she felt. Which was exactly what she wanted.

After all, *she* might have come to San Francisco with the idea of starting up an affair with her ex-husband as a way to finally get him out of her system for good, but there was no telling what he might have in mind. Once could have been enough for him. In any case, Daphne wasn't about to announce her intentions for Adam and all of Sunny's other guests to see, by giving him the skimpy black silk briefs that had been her first inclination.

Although, she thought, grinning to herself, he would have looked absolutely magnificent in them.

A ghost of a smile still hovering on her lips, Daphne got out of the car and, mindful of the height of her heels, carefully made her way up the steep incline of the street and the even steeper angle of the stairs, to the front door. Taking one last deep breath, she pasted a wide smile on her face, and rang the doorbell.

"I'll get it! I'll get it!" A high-pitched, childish voice rang out above the music. "Let me get it."

"*I'll* get it," another, older voice said. The door was yanked open. "You go back upstairs before I blister your rear," Sunny threatened cheerfully, shooing the oldest of her three children back up the wide stairs to the second floor with a careless wave of her hand.

Daphne couldn't help but notice that the nail polish on that hand was a bright orange red; almost an exact match for the silky hostess pajamas Sunny wore, and a beautiful foil for her spiky, short-cropped auburn hair.

Sunny turned toward her newly arrived guest then, a smile splitting her face from ear to ear as she saw who it was. "Daphne!" she cried, swooping to enfold her in a Giorgio-scented hug. "You look great! Elegant as all get out, dammit!" she exclaimed, standing back a little to take in Daphne's loosely belted ivory silk big shirt and shiny, form-fitting brown leather pants.

"I'm so glad you came," she said, moving in for another quick hug. "I knew you would. I told Brian—" She broke off and turned her head, raising her voice over the noise of the stereo coming from the living room. "Brian, come look who's here. It's Daphne."

Sunny's tall rangy husband, his placid gray-eyed calm the exact opposite of his wife's wacky exuberance, put his drink down on a glass side table and ambled over to greet her.

"Daphne, honey," he said warmly, cupping both her shoulders in his large square hands as he leaned down to kiss her. "It's good to see you again. Where've you been keeping yourself?"

Daphne returned his kiss warmly. "New York, mostly." She answered him literally, her eyes darting past his shoulder to the crowded room beyond. Adam wasn't anywhere to be seen. She brought her eyes back to Brian's. "Hong Kong three or four times a year to hunt for fabrics and visit the factories. Dallas and L.A. during the markets. And San Francisco every month or so." She grinned up at him. "You're just never around when I drop by."

"That's because nobody ever tells me when you're dropping by," he grumbled good-naturedly, casting a teasing eye at his wife.

"That's because you're never home," his wife grumbled back. She reached out, taking Adam's birthday present from Daphne. "Here, put this on the table with the others," she ordered, giving it to Brian.

"Yes, ma'am," he said crisply, and bowed like a hotel bell captain before he turned away to do his wife's bidding.

Sunny ignored his teasing. "I'm going to take Daphne into the living room and reintroduce her to everyone," she stated, linking her arm through Daphne's as she steered her through the open archway into the room beyond. "You remember Gail Scott, don't you, Daphne?" she said, presenting the two women to each other.

"Yes, of course, I remember Gail," Daphne replied warmly, reaching out to give the short, plump brunette a quick hug. It was enthusiastically returned. "How could I forget? Gail took me to my first women's lib meeting. Remember? At the Women's Center near the campus." She laughed a little at the memory. "God, those were the days, weren't they?" she said, and they were off, reminiscing about the "good old days."

Daphne wandered from group to group after that, reacquainting herself with the friends of her carefree, radical youth. The music throbbing from the stereo was from that era too, an eclectic mix of the Rolling Stones, Steppenwolf, the Beatles, the Beach Boys, Dylan, the Righteous Brothers, Peter, Paul and Mary. All they lacked, Daphne thought, nostalgia tugging at her heartstrings, were the love beads and headbands, poster paints and bad coffee, and someone on a soapbox spewing the political rhetoric of the day at them.

"Oh, and do you remember that 'Save the Otters' march? The one Carl arranged. It rained all over us, remember? You couldn't read the signs because the paint was dripping all over the place and the police never even bothered to show up because..."

"...that time Sunny chained herself to the door of the student union building and then lost the keys to the handcuffs and the janitor had to saw them off her. I thought I'd die laughing."

"...his van had a psychedelic paint job, remember? With exploding stars or something."

"...when we went to the all-night candlelight vigil. I'll never forget how beautiful it was. Everybody was singing and swaying."

"...Daphne was marching down Market Street in the feminists' Sunrise Protest. Remember how she hit that cameraman on the head with her sign and ended up on the six o'clock news?"

Laughter, including Daphne's own, filled the air.

"Adam got so mad I thought he'd bust a gut," another voice said.

Yes, Adam, Daphne thought. Where was he?

Someone else had apparently already asked the same question.

"I called the hospital a few minutes ago," Brian told them. "They said he was still in surgery—"

There was a unanimous groan.

"So we're going to go ahead and eat without him—"

Good-natured cheers filled the air.

Brian gave them a long-suffering look. "And he can catch up when he gets here," he finished. "So..." He bowed slightly, one arm extended in the direction of the dining room. "Food's right this way."

"No one had better lay even one finger on that cake, though," Sunny warned. "We're not cutting it until Adam gets here."

Everyone trooped toward the laden dining room table, filling up their buffet plates with triangles of shrimp toast, steamed pearl balls, finger-sized egg rolls, five spice chicken, sweet and sour pork and fluffy boiled rice. Chinese food used to be Adam's absolute favorite, Daphne remembered, reaching for a plate. Apparently, it still was.

"It's all natural," Sunny told them proudly. "Not one additive or preservative. Not a sprinkle of MSG, either."

"I can't eat it without MSG," someone deadpanned.

"Haven't you ever heard of Chinese restaurant syndrome?" Sunny began, seeing the opportunity to hold forth on one of her most dearly espoused causes: the danger of food additives in the American diet.

"At least a hundred times," teased Brian, stopping his wife before she could say another word. "Two hundred times," he exaggerated. "A thousand."

"Very funny," she said, pretending to throw a steamed pearl ball at him.

Daphne smiled at their loving byplay, filling her plate with a little bit of everything as she made her way around the table. Then, plate filled, she ambled out into the wide entry hall. Waggling the fingers of her free hand at the small redheaded child at the top of the stairs, she crossed into the living room and found herself a seat on the smooth stones of the fireplace hearth.

"So," she said a few minutes later when Sunny came in and sat down on the sofa across from her. "What have you been up to lately?"

Brian, passing by on his way to the other corner of the sofa, screwed up his face. "Don't ask," he warned.

Sunny ignored him. "Well," she began. "The kids and I are up to a mile a day."

"Just you and the kids?" Daphne slanted a teasing look at the gray-eyed man sitting at the other end of the sofa. "Not Brian, too?"

Brian shook his head. "It's a well-known medical fact that running causes shinsplints," he said in his doctor-knows-best voice.

"We don't run, we jog. Sort of," Sunny countered. "Mollie's too young to do much running."

Brian grinned. "And you're too old."

"Oh, you!" She dismissed him with an eloquent lift of her shoulder as she turned back toward Daphne. "Actually, what I've *really* been up to is something much more important," she said, and then paused significantly, her eyes flickering briefly toward her husband before she continued. "Antivivisection."

Daphne looked at her over a forkful of sweet and sour pork. "Anti-what?"

"Antivivisection," Sunny repeated, a bit more loudly.

"Oh, God," Brian groaned comically. "If you're going to start on that again I'm leaving." He made as if to stand up.

"But antivivisection is *important*," Sunny stressed, reaching out to hold him where he was.

"Of course it's important," Brian agreed, sinking back into the sofa. "Animal research has saved thousands of lives."

"That's not what I mean and you know it, Brian Andrew McCorkle!"

"Now you're really in trouble," Daphne said, grinning at him over a piece of shrimp toast. She still didn't know exactly what they were talking about—antivivisection being a word she was unfamiliar with—but she was enjoying the fireworks.

"Well, just what did you mean—" he paused, grinning at the group who had gathered round to watch the show "—*Elizabeth*."

No one, not even her parents, had called Sunny that for more years than anyone could remember. Elizabeth was Sunny's real name, but she had changed it to Sunshine during her high school, flower child days. It had been shortened to Sunny by her classmates and, suiting her far better than the more staid Elizabeth did, it had stuck.

"That was a low blow," she announced with icy dignity, but her eyes were twinkling. "Unworthy of even you."

"You started it," he pointed out. "I was merely trying to defend myself."

"Children, children," Daphne interrupted, laughing. "Before this...this *discussion* disintegrates into a full-fledged brawl, do you think one of you might explain to me what you're arguing about?"

"Antivivisection," Sunny said, as if that explained everything.

"Yes, I know but—now don't think I'm a complete idiot—but what exactly is antivivisection?"

"Antivivisection," said a voice from behind the sofa, "is the opposition of some people to the use of live animals for medical research because they believe that it causes unnecessary pain to the animal."

Daphne's eyes, as well as everyone else's, lifted toward the speaker. She saw a tall slim woman of, perhaps, twenty-three or twenty-four years of age. Her heavy, straight blond hair was cut shoulder length and held back from her face with a comb on either side. Something about her intensely blue eyes and the way she held her head was vaguely familiar, but Daphne couldn't quite place her. She was much too young to be part of the old "gang" and too old to be the daughter of one of them, either. Still, Daphne had the nagging feeling that she knew her.

"But it does cause pain!" Sunny was saying, her voice passionate with outrage. "Great pain."

"Yes, I suppose it does." The young woman spoke in a cool and detached manner. "But not *unnecessary* pain. How else are we going to find a cure for all the hundreds of diseases that man is heir to?"

"I don't know. But butchering innocent animals isn't the way."

"Really, Mrs. McCorkel," the young woman said dryly, her expression faintly disdainful. "No one 'butchers' innocent animals. Every care is taken to see that the animal doesn't suffer any more than absolutely necessary."

"But the animals still suffer horribly." She shuddered. "They give them cancer and other awful, crippling, painful diseases. They do things to their brains and their hearts. They—"

"Sunny," Brian said kindly, putting a hand on his wife's arm. "I don't think a birthday party is the place to discuss this sort of thing. Leave it be."

"But—"

"Leave it be," he repeated softly.

Sunny looked down at her lap for a moment, and Daphne saw her shoulders lift in a sigh. Then she raised her head, and there was a smile on her face. "Brian's right. This is no place for that kind of discussion." She jumped up from the sofa, "If everybody's finished eating, let's push back the furniture and dance." She picked up her plate from the coffee table with one hand and reached across for Daphne's with the other. "I'll just take a few of these things out to the kitchen first. You all start moving the furniture." She turned swiftly, disappearing through the open archway, into the dining room and beyond.

Daphne rose from her spot on the hearth as some of the others began to do as Sunny had suggested, and approached the young woman who had defended the practice of vivisection so coolly. "I know this is going to sound like a line from an old movie," she began, smiling, "but don't I know you?"

"You used to," the younger woman said. She paused, a cool unfriendly smile turning up her perfect pink lips. "I'm Marcia Forrest."

Daphne stared at her blankly for a moment.

"Adam's sister," she elaborated.

"Oh, my God, of course! Marcia. No wonder you looked so familiar." *And are so unfriendly*, Daphne thought. Adam's baby sister had never liked Adam's wife. "The last time I saw you, you were what? Twelve? Thirteen?"

"Thirteen," Marcia acknowledged, making no effort to help the conversation along.

"So, what are you up to these days?"

"I'm in my second year of medical school at UC San Francisco."

Adam's alma mater, Daphne thought. "Oh, you're planning to be a doctor, then."

"A surgeon," Marcia corrected.

"Making plastic surgery your speciality, too?" Plastic surgery, with an emphasis on severe burn cases, was Adam's speciality.

"No," Marcia said shortly. "I intend to specialize in cardiovascular surgery. Surgery on the heart," she added, as if Daphne might not know what it was.

"How . . . admirable. Adam must be very proud of you," Daphne said sincerely.

"Yes, I believe he is," Marcia said, just a bit too smugly.

"Well, it was nice talking to you again but if you'll excuse me—" Daphne gestured in the direction of the dining room "I—think I'll just go see if Sunny needs any help." She hurried off to the kitchen.

"Marcia Forrest certainly has a charming bedside manner, doesn't she?" Daphne said a few minutes later, as she stood at the sink, helping Sunny scrape plates before loading them into the dishwasher.

"The original Miss Iceberg," the redhead agreed dryly. She looked up from what she was doing for a moment, a wicked smile on her face. "I take it she still worships the ground you walk on?"

Daphne flicked a wet hand in Sunny's direction. "Very funny," she said, and then sighed. "That girl has never liked me. Not from day one, when she was hardly more than ten years old. I wonder why?"

"Because Adam did—and still does—*like* you, that's why."

"Jealousy, you mean?" Daphne said, ignoring the bit about Adam still liking her and the stress that Sunny had placed on the word.

"Well, of course. What else would you expect. Adam is her adored older brother, and halfway to sainthood as far as she's concerned. The first one in the family to go to college and make something of himself." Sunny babbled on, rinsing the dishes that Daphne had scraped before sticking them into the dishwasher. "He's helping put her through med school, did you know that? Which, of course, makes him even more godlike in her eyes."

Daphne nodded. "He always wanted to help his family." She paused for a moment, remembering. "It always made him so... so *angry* with himself that he couldn't afford to help his younger brothers with their educations."

Sunny shrugged. "They did all right without his help."

"And what did they end up doing? The other two boys?"

Sunny smiled. "They're hardly boys anymore," she reminded Daphne. "John does something scientific involving the coral reefs around Hawaii. And David is an accountant. Lives in Phoenix, Arizona, with his wife and two kids."

"And Gracie and Art? How are they?" Daphne asked, referring to Adam's parents. "As I remember, they weren't all that crazy about me, either." Her eyebrows quirked upward. "I'm sure they thought I was going to lead their future doctor away from the straight and narrow."

"They're fine, too, as far as I know," Sunny told her, pouring dishwashing detergent into the proper receptacle. "Still living in the old neighborhood, even though Adam was all prepared to buy them a big new house. Didn't want to leave their friends, apparently. But they did accept a trip to Hawaii last summer. As an anniversary present."

"That must have made Adam happy."

"Tickled him pink," Sunny agreed. She shut the door to the dishwasher and pushed the On button with the knuckle of her index finger. Turning around, she crossed her arms and leaned back against the kitchen counter.

"Do you know," she said reflectively, "that this is the first—the *very* first—time I've even heard you willingly mention Adam's name since the divorce."

"Is it?"

"Yes," Sunny said softly. "Why is that, I wonder?"

"Because," Daphne replied firmly, "this will be the first time I've seen him since the divorce, that's why. Well, not counting the, uh, Children's charity thing, that is. Since he's... he's back in the Bay Area now I'll probably run into him once in a while. Here, if no place else and, well, it's only sensible to try to be civil to each other."

"Hmm," was all Sunny would say. Then, she cocked her head slightly, listening. "Well, I guess you'd better prepare to be civil. I think I hear Adam's voice in the front hall."

Daphne followed her friend out of the kitchen, hanging back as Sunny hurried up to greet her latest guest, watching as Adam bent his head to kiss Sunny's proffered cheek. He looked a little tired, she thought, but, then, who wouldn't after standing through hours of surgery? The hint of fatigue around his eyes and mouth in no way detracted from his golden good looks, and even without the tuxedo he was devastating. The polish he had acquired was not just a surface thing, she realized, drinking in the sight of him in his tan slacks and tweedy brown blazer. He had an indefinable something about him that went bone deep. It drew her eyes like a magnet.

He laughed at something that Sunny said, his eyes crinkling up at the corners, and extended his hand toward Brian. The two men exchanged a warm handshake and another quick grip that made Adam laugh again, and then he moved away from the door to greet Marcia with a brief, brotherly hug.

"I take it you knew about this little surprise," he said with mock severity.

Marcia nodded, obviously well pleased with herself. "Of course. How else do you think I could make sure that Ginny would get you here, come hell or high water?"

"So, Ginny was in on this, too, hmm?" He glanced back over his shoulder. "Well, come here and take your medicine, woman." He reached a long arm out behind him, circling the shoulders of a small, dark-haired woman, and hauled her up, laughing, to stand at his side. As he turned back to his sister, still smiling at the surprise they pulled on him, he caught sight of Daphne standing in the open archway.

He went stock-still for a moment, his eyes on hers as the quick color came and went in his face, but Daphne wasn't looking at him. She was looking, instead, at the woman who stood so securely in the circle of his arm, her fingers curved into the tweedy material at his lean waist.

She was dark-haired and dark-eyed and her full smiling lips were colored a soft becoming red. Her navy sheath dress was more classic than fashionable and it covered a body that was slim-hipped, small-breasted and long-legged. She was, Daphne thought despairingly, quite lovely.

And Adam had his arm around her.

Daphne felt all her plans go down the drain as surely as if someone had suddenly pulled a plug on them. It just hadn't occurred to her that Adam—*her* Adam—might have another woman. Not after the night in her hotel room.

Her eyes lifted to his face then, a half-accusing expression in their golden-brown depths as she stared at him. Adam stared back, seemingly as unable as she to look away. His blue eyes were full of wariness, she thought, as if he were afraid she might tell the whole room, and the woman by his side, what had happened between them the night of the charity dance.

Well, don't worry, she telegraphed silently, her pride stung. *I want to keep it a secret as much as you do.*

The exchange of glances lasted only a second or two, the duration of a heartbeat only, but everyone in the room seemed to be holding their breath, waiting for what would happen next.

And what happened next was that Daphne smiled, a lovely, warm, utterly false smile, and crossed the room to stand in front of her ex-husband. "Happy birthday, Adam," she said evenly, extending her right hand as she spoke.

He took her hand, his fingers clamping down on hers. "Thank you," he answered, his voice just as even and apparently unemotional as hers.

And, then, their hands dropped back to their sides and they stood there like two people who had never been more than casual friends. Everyone seemed to let their breath out as the hoped-for explosion fizzled out, and they all started talking at once, wandering back in the direction of the living room or the dining room or down the hall to the bathroom. Even Sunny went, covertly dragged away by Brian.

"Aren't you going to introduce Ginny to Daphne?" Marcia prompted when Adam made no move to do so.

"What?" He shook his head slightly as if coming out of a trance and met his sister's eyes. "Oh, sure. Sure." He glanced from Daphne to the woman at his side. "Ginny Phelps meet Daphne Granger," he said stiffly, adding no more information than that.

The two women nodded at each other, exchanging cool smiles, neither of them sure of the status of the other in Adam's life.

Marcia was quick to fill in the gaps. "Ginny is a nurse. The best OR nurse he's ever worked with, Adam says." She looked up at her brother. "Isn't that right, Adam?"

"Yes." He gave Ginny's shoulders a halfhearted little squeeze and dropped his arm. "The best," he added, running one hand through the hair that fell across his forehead.

"They've been a team practically since the day Adam started at Children's." She shot a quick look at Daphne to see if the message was getting across. It was. "Adam hates to have to work with anyone but Ginny," she continued. "And—"

"Marcia, please," Ginny interrupted, laughing a little self-consciously. "You're making me blush."

"Sorry," Marcia said, but she didn't look sorry. She looked like the cat who had just cornered the market on canaries.

"Well, it's been lovely to meet you, Ginny," Daphne said then. "And so nice to see you again, Adam. And you too, Marcia," she added insincerely. "But, if you'll excuse me, I have to go find Sunny and say my goodbyes."

"You're not leaving already?" It was Marcia, not Adam, who made the required protest. Her tone was victorious.

"'Fraid so. I've been here longer than I'd planned already. I told Sunny I'd try to stop by for just a few minutes and—" her shoulders lifted in a little shrug "—well, you know how it is. We got to talking over the 'good old days' and the time just slipped away. I've got an early meeting at I. Magnin tomorrow," she lied. "And, unfortunately, I need to go over my presentation one more time." She glanced toward the living room as she spoke, her expression silently informing her hostess that she was about to leave.

Sunny came hurrying out to stop her. "You're not leaving already?" she said, meaning it far more than Marcia had. She glanced up at Adam. "Not when the guest of honor just got here."

"'Fraid so," she said again. "But it can't be helped. Now, Sunny," she continued when her friend would have made another protest, "I've already stayed much longer than I'd planned. I really have to be going."

"Well." Sunny's voice was little-girl sulky. "If you have to." She sighed theatrically. "Where's your purse?"

Daphne touched the back pocket of her leather pants. It held a car key, a credit card and a ten-dollar bill. "Right here."

"How 'bout your coat? Did you come in with a coat?"

"I didn't wear one. No." She stopped Sunny as she raised her hand to summon Brian. "Don't bother Brian, he's busy. Just say goodbye for me, okay? And tell him I'll see him next time I'm in town."

The two women exchanged a quick, warm hug. "Drive carefully," Sunny admonished.

"I will." She raised her eyes to Adam's one last time. "Happy birthday," she said and hurried out into the foggy night without waiting for his reply.

7

DAPHNE WAS WIDE AWAKE when the first pale fingers of sunlight started to pry their way around the edges of the blue brocade drapes of her hotel room. She lay on her back on the rumpled double bed closest to the window, one hand flung above her head, the other clutching a soggy tissue against the front of her ivory nightgown. She stared up at the ceiling, eyes dry now, thinking about the night before.

She was glad, she told herself fiercely, trying to believe it, *glad* that Adam had come to Sunny's party with another woman. It had kept her from making a complete fool of herself. Kept her from even attempting to start some damned, doomed, idiotic affair with him.

Which was a good thing, she thought, sniffling slightly, because she wouldn't have known how to start one, anyway, despite her intentions. What would she have said to him if he *had* come alone?

Elaine had suggested that she be straightforward and up-front. "Just tell him what you have in mind. Say 'Listen, Adam, I enjoyed the other night, let's do it again soon.' He'll take it from there," she'd promised.

But Daphne couldn't have said those words, or anything like them, in a million years. What she'd had in mind was something a bit more subtle. Invite him out for a birthday drink, maybe, and then let nature take its course. Yet, both of those alternatives sounded so...so calculating and

Daphne was a woman who had always expressed her emotions more spontaneously.

Well, it was a moot point now. She might as well stop wasting her time thinking about what might have been and deal with what was.

Besides, it wouldn't have worked, anyway. There was no way on earth that she was ever going to get over Adam, no way she was ever going to "get him out of her system," no matter what Elaine or a hundred magazine articles said. To expose herself to more heartache by trying was foolish in the extreme.

She had lived the last eleven years of her life without him, she told herself firmly, she could live the rest of her life without him, too.

The thought brought a lump to her throat and tears to her golden-brown eyes. She blinked them back stubbornly, ordering them not to fall, and then sat up, switched on the bedside lamp and reached for the telephone. She was leaving San Francisco today—now—on the first available flight and to hell with I. Magnin and her other accounts. Elaine could fly out and handle them. She knew the business as well as Daphne did and it was high time Daphne started letting her assistant handle more things on her own. She had been meaning to do just that for months.

The phone rang just as Daphne put her hand on it and she jumped, starting back as if she had been burned. Who, she wondered, would be calling at this hour? It was barely past six o'clock. Not even Sunny, who would want to lecture her for leaving so soon after Adam had arrived, would be awake this early. She let it ring three times before finally picking it up.

"Hello?" she said, her husky voice made even huskier by the tears shed during a sleepless night.

"Daffy?" The voice on the other end was achingly familiar. "It's Adam. Did I wake you?"

"No. No, you didn't wake me," she said, startled to hear from him after spending all night thinking about the man. It was almost as if she had conjured him up. "I've been awake all—" She started to say "all night." "For at least an hour," she amended. "Is there something I can do for you?" she said when he remained silent.

"Well, I thought...that is, we didn't get much of a chance to visit with each other last night. And I thought you might have time for breakfast before your business meeting." His voice was appealingly hesitant, like a little boy asking for something he wanted very much but wasn't sure he was going to get.

"Meeting?" Daphne said, forgetting for a moment that had been her excuse to leave the party last night. Comprehension dawned. "Oh, the meeting at I. Magnin. Yes, well, it's not for several hours yet." Actually, it wasn't until Monday. "But I—"

"Then you're free for breakfast," Adam said eagerly, not giving her a chance to refuse.

"Well, yes, but—"

Adam interrupted her again. "I'd really like to talk to you," he said, his voice low.

She knew she should refuse. Seeing him again was just asking for trouble. Besides, she had already decided that the best thing for her was to go back to New York *without* seeing him again. Hadn't she?

"Daffy?"

Oh, God, it wasn't fair that he could do this to her with just the sound of his voice. It just wasn't fair! "Where shall I meet you?" she said, as surprised as he was to hear the words coming out of her mouth.

"You stay where you are. I'll be right up."

"Up?" she squeaked. "You mean you're in the hotel?"

"At a house phone in the lobby."

"Fine, then you stay—" she began, intending to tell him that he should remain where he was and she'd come down. But it was too late. He had hung up on the word "fine."

Oh, my God, she thought. Adam was on his way to her room! And she wasn't dressed, hadn't combed her hair, and her eyes . . . her eyes were all red from crying half the night.

She snatched her velour robe off the floor by the bed and stepped into it, zipping it up as she hurried toward the bathroom. *Lord, what a mess,* she thought, leaning forward to peer at herself in the mirror over the basin. She brushed her teeth first and then bent low over the sink, scooping handfuls of cold water over her face.

Better, she decided, peering into the mirror again, *but not good enough.* Her nose and the delicate skin around her eyes still looked suspiciously pink. She rummaged through her makeup case, found her powder and brush, and dusted it across her face with quick, nervous strokes. A bit of mascara was next and then just a dab of lip gloss . . .

There was a sharp rap on the door.

Daphne started, smearing lip gloss all across one cheek, and the lip brush fell to the tiled counter. "Just a minute," she called, hoping she sounded more in control than she felt, knowing she didn't.

She yanked a tissue from the dispenser in the bathroom wall and carefully wiped off the smeared gloss. With shaking fingers, she started to apply another coat.

There was another rap on the door.

"Damn." She threw the lip brush down in exasperation. Better he didn't think she had made an effort, anyway. "I'm coming!" she hollered, eyes on the mirror as she ran both hands through the wisps of unbrushed hair that clung to her forehead and temples, fluffing them up as best she could.

"Oh, the hell with it," she muttered, seeing how little improvement it made. Waving a dismissive hand at her image, she left the bathroom.

The rumpled bed caught her eye as she headed for the door. Oh, no, the bed. It was unmade. Suggestive. She flew across the room, snapping on the overhead light as she went, and pulled the bedspread up over the pillows, trying to smooth it into some sort of respectable order.

Another rap, louder and more impatient.

"I'm coming, I said!" *Impatient as ever*, she thought, as she reached for the door. She put her hand on the doorknob, took a deep steadying breath, arranged her lips in what she hoped was a casual smile, and opened it.

"Adam," she began brightly and then stopped, not knowing what else to say.

He was dressed the way she had always liked best, casually, in a pair of faded jeans, a dark periwinkle-blue turtleneck that intensified the color of his eyes and enhanced the golden glow of his skin, and a Sam Spade trench coat with the collar turned up. His smooth-shaven cheeks were slightly flushed from the morning cold, his blond hair slightly windblown by the ever-present breezes that whipped in off of the bay. Dressed this way, standing there with a white waxed-paper sack in one hand, he quite literally took her breath away.

Oh, Adam!

"May I come in?"

"Please do." Daphne inclined her head and stepped back to allow him entrance. "You'll have to forgive how it looks in here," she said nervously, stooping to pick up a satin teddy from the floor. She tossed it into the open suitcase on top of the unused bed.

"Still don't believe in housework, huh?" he teased, setting the paper sack down on the small round table in front of the draped window.

"Oh, I believe in it now," Daphne said. "I just don't do it any better."

"So I see." He plucked a pale yellow wisp of a bra off the table and handed it to her. "Wouldn't want to spill coffee on it," he said, grinning when she snatched it out of his fingers and threw it on the bed behind her. He opened the sack, releasing the fragrant steam from the coffee inside. "Do you still like raspberry danish?"

"You've got raspberry danish in there, too?"

"Too?" he inquired, prying the lid off a large Styrofoam cup.

"As well as coffee."

"Sure." He held the cup of coffee toward her, waiting until she took it. "Coffee's no good without something to dunk in it." He pried the lid off a second cup and took a sip before setting it aside. "Here. A raspberry danish for you." He handed it to her. "A cinnamon roll for me and—" he pulled out two more covered plastic cups "—orange juice for both of us. Well, come on, sit down." He motioned toward the chair on the other side of the table. "Eat before it gets cold."

"The danish isn't going to get any colder than it already is," Daphne pointed out, but she sat, anyway.

Adam shrugged out of his trench coat, draping it across the back of the chair, and sat down, too. "So eat it before it gets hot then," he said, peeling the foil lids off the cups of orange juice. He slid one across the table and handed her a napkin. "Shall I open these?" he asked, nodding toward the drapes.

Daphne, her mouth full of raspberry danish, shook her head. "Too bright," she mumbled, thinking of her unmade-up face and finger-combed hair. She took a sip of her coffee to wash down the slightly stale pastry. "So." She glanced at Adam from under her lashes. "You said you wanted to talk. What about?"

Adam shrugged uneasily, eyes downcast as he pretended interest in the cinnamon roll on the napkin in front of him. "About the other night," he said, and took a quick gulp of his coffee.

"Last night?" Her forehead wrinkled in a frown. "What about last night?"

"No, not *last* night." He looked up, capturing her eyes with his. "The night of Sunny's charity thing."

"Oh. *That* other night." Daphne forced herself to hold his eyes. Nothing like coming right to the point, she thought. She forced herself to sound blithely unconcerned. "What about it?"

"I wanted to apologize." Each word sounded as if it were being yanked out of him with a pair of forceps.

Daphne took a quick sip of her coffee. "For what?" she asked, but she didn't really want to know. She didn't want to hear him say how sorry he was that he had made love to her. Not when it was the most beautiful thing that had happened to her in a long, long time.

"For leaving you so abruptly like that. I didn't...I mean, it wasn't—" He looked down again, tearing at his roll as he searched for a word. "It wasn't polite," he said finally, looking up to see how she was taking it.

She took it quite well. *Not polite*, she thought, wondering if that's all that was bothering him; a breach in the etiquette of brief sexual encounters. "Well, don't worry about it," she said lightly, as if to show him how little it mattered. "You had an emergency, so you're excused." She smiled across the rim of her cup: a false, brittle smile. "Feel better now?" she asked, taking a sip.

"No." The words were intense. Forceful. Bleak.

Daphne's eyebrows rose. "No?"

"I didn't want to leave you that night." He reached across the table and put his hand on her arm. His fingers seemed to burn right through the sleeve of her robe. "I wanted to stay and make love to you again. Slowly, all night long. In every way possible." His hand tightened, melting the fabric, melting Daphne. She began to feel faint. "I still want to," he said quietly.

Daphne closed her eyes for a moment fighting the weakness that had invaded her body at his touch, fighting the temptation of his words. Fighting... What was it she had told herself? Oh, yes. It wouldn't work. She opened her eyes and eased her arm out from under his hand. "You didn't call," she accused, surprising herself. It was the last thing she had intended to say.

Adam let her pull away. "I wanted to." He ran his hand through his hair. "God, how I wanted to! But I thought it would be better—for both of us—if I didn't." He began tearing at the hapless cinnamon roll again, reducing it to crumbs. "We've got separate lives now," he went on, half speaking to himself. "*Successful* lives," he emphasized, "on separate coasts. And it's been eleven years. We've gotten along fine—just fine—without each other for eleven goddamn years." He looked up, his eyes faintly accusing as if it were all her fault. "I actually thought I was over you. Over wanting you," he amended. "But you're like a fever. Like a..." He shook his head, looking as confused as she felt, and ran his hand through his hair again. "Like a drug to me, Daphne. And all I have to do is see you again and I ache like a sixteen-year-old boy who hasn't had his first woman." He took a deep breath and dropped his hand to the table. "Why the *hell* did you have to come back here?"

"Because I ache for you, too," she said simply.

She knew, even as she said it, that it was probably unwise to admit how she felt. But she knew it must have been hard for him to lay his feelings out in the open and, knowing that, she could be no less open about hers. She wasn't being *precisely* honest, perhaps, because her feelings went far deeper than just a physical ache, but her statement was honest as far as it went.

"You, too?" Adam's hand reached out again, tentatively touching hers where it lay on the table.

"Me, too." She lifted her hand, palm toward him, and let him lace his fingers with hers. "After that night I couldn't get you out of my mind. Couldn't forget how good it had been." His fingers tightened. She squeezed back. "I told myself it would be best if we didn't see each other again. That it was just a temporary...aberration, and it would go away if I ignored it. But then Sunny called and invited me to your birthday party and I thought 'Why not?' We're both adults now, not two crazy kids. We could be friends. Lots of ex's are friends. Right?"

Adam nodded slowly, his expression wary.

Oh, hell! Who am I trying to kid, she thought, seeing it. *Adam? Or myself?*

She straightened and pulled her hand from his. "No, that's not true." She laced her fingers together on the table. "The truth is," she said, staring down at her hands, "that I quite cold-bloodedly decided to come to Sunny's party to start an affair with you."

"What?" Adam's blue eyes opened wide.

"An affair." She glanced at him from under the sweep of her lashes. "You know, two people meeting over a period of time for illicit sexual purposes?"

"Yes, I know what it is. What I don't know is why you'd want to have one."

"Well, I thought . . . that is." She lifted her head and met his eyes straight on. "I thought having an affair with you would be the way to sort of, you know, get you out of my system. I mean, this intense . . . *thing* we seem to have for each other would have to fizzle out sooner or later and—"

"It hasn't fizzled in eleven years."

"No, but I think that's because of the way it ended. It was so abrupt and the . . . the . . ." She stumbled over the word, knowing love was the right one but not willing to go that far. "The passion never had a chance to die a natural death. We parted still wanting each other physically, even though the emotions were gone." *On your part, anyway,* she added silently. "And I thought, if we had an affair it might, uh, might—"

"Get me out of your system for good," he finished for her. His tone was tinged with hurt but Daphne didn't notice.

She nodded, completely forgetting that she had spent most of last night deciding that *nothing* was going to get Adam out of her system for good. "Yes." She smiled ruefully. "Do I sound totally crazy?"

"Maybe. But if you're crazy, then so am I."

"Huh?" Daphne said inelegantly. She had expected him to agree with her because it *was* a crazy idea. She knew that. So should he.

"I said 'But if you're crazy, then—'"

"No, that's not what I meant. I mean, I know *what* you said. What I meant was, what did you mean?"

He gave her that slow sleepy smile. The one that turned her insides to jelly. "Huh?" he said, teasing her.

She gave him a look and made as if to throw the rest of her uneaten raspberry danish at him.

"Okay, okay." He held up his hand, palm out, as if to ward off a blow. "What I meant was, well . . ." His smile turned rueful and he dropped his hand. "I agree."

Daphne lifted her brows inquiringly.

"I think we should have an affair," he elaborated.

"Oh."

They both fell silent, picking at their respective pastries.

Daphne spoke up after a minute. "Well," she said a bit breathlessly. "Should we start now?"

"Start what?"

"Oh, for God's sake, Adam," she said, exasperated with all this pussyfooting around. They were adults, weren't they? "Our affair."

Adam grinned self-consciously. "Oh, that. Sure." He stood up and brushed his hands off against the seat of his jeans. Reaching across the remains of their uneaten breakfast, he lifted her out of her chair by the shoulders and eased her around the table, maneuvering her pliant body toward his.

Daphne closed her eyes, head tilted back as she waited for his kiss. It didn't come. She opened her eyes.

"What about your appointment?" Adam asked, his hands gripping her shoulders as he gazed down into her upturned face.

Daphne blinked. "What appointment?"

"The one with I. Magnin."

"Oh, *that* appointment." She paused, considering. "There isn't one," she said, deciding to tell the truth. "Well, that is, there *is* one but it isn't until Monday."

"Not this morning?" Adam thought about that for a moment, his blue eyes holding hers. "You mean you lied?"

"I didn't *lie*." Daphne wiggled out from under his hands. "I just rearranged the facts a little." Her brows arched, disappearing into the tangle of curls on her forehead. "Don't you ever rearrange the facts, Adam?"

"Why did you feel it necessary to, um—" his lips turned up at her choice of words "—rearrange the facts?"

"Because you came to Sunny's party with that—" she hesitated, fighting the urge to give in to bitchiness "—that friend of yours, that's why."

"Friend of mine?" His brow wrinkled for a moment. "Oh, you mean Ginny. What's Ginny got to do with it?"

Lord, how could he be so dumb! Did she really have to spell it out for him? Apparently, she did. She sat down on the edge of the bed and picked at nonexistent lint on the lap of her velour robe.

"Because, when I realized that you and Ginny were a couple my little plan for, uh, for..." She hesitated, not wanting to say the word, and then went ahead. It had already been said, anyway, so what difference did it make? "My plan for an affair suddenly didn't seem to be the smartest thing I'd ever come up with. The 'other woman' is *not* a role I'm particularly interested in playing. Even for you." *Oh, no! Had she really said that?* She went on hurriedly. "I needed a reason to leave gracefully and the meeting with I. Magnin was the best I could come up with on such short notice." She looked up at him through her lashes. "Satisfied?"

"No." Adam sat down on the bed next to her and took her chin in his hand, turning her head to face him. "Ginny and I are not a couple," he said, stressing every word as his eyes blazed into hers. "If we were I wouldn't be here. Is that clear?" He shook her chin lightly when she didn't answer. "Yes or no?"

"Yes, Adam," she replied meekly, something inside of her flaming into sudden joy. *Ginny and I are not a couple!* Had he ever said seven more beautiful words to her?

"Good." His hand feathered down to caress her throat. "Now, if that's settled, can we get back to what we were doing?"

A slow grin spread over Daphne's face. "And what was that? Eating that sorry excuse for a breakfast?"

Adam shook his head, his lips quirking up into an answering grin. "There's the little matter of our affair. I thought we'd start with, say, a little heavy necking." He leaned toward her, his body pressing hers back against the rumpled bed. "A bit of serious petting, then—"

Daphne's stomach growled loudly, a low complaining rumble that seemed to go on for several seconds.

Adam groaned comically and stopped advancing.

"Just ignore it," Daphne advised, reaching up to pull his head down to hers.

Their lips touched.

Daphne's stomach growled again.

Adam sighed and sat up. "Come on, get up." He stood, pulling her to her feet. "I refuse to make love to a woman who's stomach is growling at me."

"But Adam," Daphne began, her voice rich with disappointment.

He stopped her words with a quick, hard kiss, both hands cradling her face. "The next time I make love to you, Daffy," he said clearly, staring down into her eyes, "it's going to take a good long time. Not ten minutes like the other night. Hours," he promised gruffly and kissed her again, lighter this time. "I intend to savour every luscious inch of you and I don't want you fainting from hunger right in the middle of it. So . . ." He released her with a last quick kiss on the end of her nose and turned her toward the bathroom. "You go get dressed and I'll take you out for a real breakfast. Okay?"

"Okay," she said reluctantly, allowing herself to be propelled away from him. She paused by the open suitcase on the other bed to fish out some suitable clothes and then, tossing them over her arm, she disappeared into the bathroom.

She showered quickly, thanking current fashion for the fact that she had hair that could be washed and styled in less than twenty minutes. Using a blow-dryer and her fingers, she fluffed the feathery golden-brown curls into order around her forehead and temples, teasing seemingly artless wisps to cling to the nape of her long elegant neck. Her makeup took as little time. A dab of sheer ivory foundation, a dusting of peachy blusher, was all her complexion needed to make it glow.

She had never looked better in her life, she thought, deftly applying the ivory and brown shadows that would make her eyes appear even larger than they already were. That's what love did for a woman. It made her sparkle as if she were lit from inside by a thousand candles.

Resolutely, like a child who refuses to think about the punishment that will come at the end of a forbidden act, Daphne pushed all thoughts of tomorrow firmly out of her mind. She was happy now. Deliriously, insanely, deliciously, giddily happy for the first time in years.

Oh, it was true that her business gave her a great deal of happiness—it was something she had always, and would always, want and need—but that happiness was completely different from the feeling that was coursing through her now.

And it was true that she had found a mild sort of happiness with Miles. More friends than lovers, they had drifted along in a sort of placid contentment, sailing through their life together as if it were a small sheltered lake, protected from even the mildest emotional storms. There had been no highs with Miles, no lows and, thus, no excitement.

Being with Adam, though, was like being out on the bay on an especially windy day. Exhilarating, challenging, exciting—and just the tiniest bit frightening.

No, she amended. No, it was more than a tiny bit frightening. It was terrifying. What if he set her adrift again before she was ready?

And he would, she told herself, staring wide-eyed at the woman in the mirror. That had to be faced up front. Because Adam would eventually get her "out of his system" and she would be left alone again, still loving him.

"So what else is new?" she murmured.

She had loved Adam since she was seventeen years old. And had continued loving him, in absentia so to speak, since she was twenty. She had survived it then—and even gone on to make a success of her life—she would survive it when it happened again. As it surely would. But until then... until then, she told herself, she would enjoy every minute of every day with him and not think about the future. They were going to have a glorious affair. Simply glorious!

She finished making up her face and dressed quickly, stepping into a sleek-fitting peach silk teddy before wiggling into the same tight, brown leather pants she had worn to Sunny's party. She pulled an oversized, bulky-knit butterscotch-colored sweater over her head. It had a high cowl neck that nestled under her chin, long loose sleeves meant to be worn pushed up, and a hem that ended halfway down her thighs. She hitched it up a bit with a wide, woven-leather belt that buckled over her left hipbone.

Satisfied with her appearance, she opened the bathroom door to find Adam sprawled out across the bed, arms folded under his head as he watched the Roadrunner make mincemeat out of Wily Coyote.

"Very highbrow stuff you're watching there," she commented, flicking a hand at the television screen. She began digging around in her suitcase for a pair of knee-socks.

Adam grinned at her from the bed. "Hey, these are classics. Besides, there's nothing else on TV on Saturday mornings."

"Brain candy," she said dismissively. "Known to cause severe cavities in the cerebral cortex," Daphne informed him, sitting down on the edge of the bed to pull on her socks.

"'Zat so?" he said, ignoring her.

"Umm." Daphne stomped her feet into leather half boots that matched her sweater and stood up, walking across the room to the dresser. Rummaging through an open vanity case, she picked out a pair of shiny bronze metal discs set with gleaming tiger's eye. "And, according to Sunny, cartoons are also thought to encourage violence in children," she said, watching Adam in the mirror as she inserted the earrings into her pierced ears.

"It's okay," Adam assured her, laughing as Wily Coyote was launched into space on a keg of dynamite. "I'm not a child."

Daphne's eyebrows rose. "Says who?"

"Whom," Adam corrected, jackknifing up from the bed to turn off the television. His eyes ran up and down her slender form. "You look like a ragamuffin," he said, his eyes approving. "A very sexy, elegant little ragamuffin but—"

"I'll have you know, Dr. Forrest," she interrupted, pretending indignation, "that this is a highly expensive, original design."

"One of yours?"

Daphne shook her head. "Unfortunately, no. I only do evening clothes." She picked up her bag, a rich brown suede hobo big enough to hold a week's worth of clothes, and slung it over her shoulder. "Well, I'm ready." She arched an eyebrow at him as she headed for the door. "Let's get breakfast out of the way, shall we?" Her grin was lascivious. "I'm starving."

8

"YOU'RE SURE YOU DON'T MIND?" Adam asked again as he pulled the dark green BMW into his designated parking place in the lot at Children's Hospital. "You could take the car to my place and wait for me there if you'd rather. I can always grab a taxi."

"No, I don't mind, Adam," she told him for the fourth time. "Honest. Besides, how long could it to take to check on one patient? Fifteen minutes?"

"At least thirty," Adam said truthfully. "Maybe more, depending."

"Depending on what?"

"On how she's feeling, mainly. How much pain she's in. If she's restive or fretful or needs a little extra cheering up." He lifted his shoulders in a small shrug as he reached to set the parking brake. "Whether or not her mother's there and wants to talk to me. Any number of things." He turned toward her, a look of concern on his face. "Are you sure you don't mind waiting?"

"I'm sure," she said firmly. As long as he smiled at her like that she wouldn't mind anything. "After the way we've been running around all day, it'll be a pleasure to sit down with a cup of coffee for a few minutes."

"You say that because you haven't tasted hospital coffee."

"It can't be any worse than the stuff I make myself. And, besides, if I have a bad reaction, I'm in a hospital, right?"

"Right," he agreed, opening his door. Then, before Daphne could do it herself, he came around to the passenger door and was reaching down a hand to help her out.

He let it go as they entered the hospital, though, and took her elbow instead as he guided her to a nurses' station. The nurse on duty, a fiftyish bright-eyed brunette, looked up at the sound of their footsteps, a wide smile replacing the professionally polite expression on her face as she saw who was approaching.

"Dr. Forrest," she said, standing practically at attention as he came up to the counter that separated the nurses' station from the rest of the wide hall.

"Hello, Peg." Adam returned her smile warmly. "How's it going?"

"Fine. Been quiet as a tomb for the last hour."

"Ah, so they're letting you catch up on your reading." He glanced at Daphne. "Peg is addicted to detective thrillers. The gorier, the better." He looked back at the plump, dark-haired nurse, affection in his blue eyes. "What is it tonight? Clive Cussler?" He leaned over the counter to read the title of the paperback that was lying facedown on the desk. "Micky Spillane?"

"Travis McGee." She flashed him an impish grin. "I'll lend it to you when I'm finished."

"Thanks, but I don't think my nerves can take it." He shuddered theatrically, hunching his shoulders like a child. "All that blood." His eyes were twinkling.

Daphne's eyes widened with surprise. She had never known Adam to make even the smallest joke in connection with his work, no matter how harmless. He had always treated it with the utmost seriousness. Unlike other med students, he had never been one to indulge in "bedpan humor" or make ghoulish jokes about cadavers. Apparently, he had changed. Oh, not that he would ever make those sorts of jokes. Medicine was too close to a holy calling to him for that, but he had obviously mellowed enough to tease about it.

"Tell me another funny story," Peg snorted. She flapped her hand at Adam in a dismissive gesture and then reached down and pushed the book aside. "Now, Dr. Forrest," she said, suddenly all starched efficiency. "I know you didn't just drop by to discuss my great taste in literature. So..." She ran a quick eye down the list on her desk. "The little Jenkins girl?"

Adam nodded, all business, too. "Any problems?"

"Not a one, doctor. I gave her the medication you ordered about—" she glanced at her watch "—*exactly* twenty-two minutes ago and she seems to be resting comfortably." Quickly, Peg shuffled through the free-standing file on her desk and handed him a manila folder attached to a metal clipboard. The name, Jenkins, Tiffany, was typed on the label.

Adam flipped it open and began scanning the topmost page. "Was she fussy today? Complaining of pain? Anything?"

Peg shook her head. "She's been her same quiet little self. Either sleeping or just lying in her bed, staring up at the butterfly mural on the ceiling with those big brown eyes of hers. Breaks my heart to see a child so accepting of pain," she commented idly. "I'd almost rather hear them hollering."

"I know what you mean." Adam nodded, acknowledging her observations while he continued to peruse the file. "Little Tiffany has had more than her share of pain in the past few months." He sighed and another kind of pain, a sadness at his own inability to ease his patient's suffering, flickered across his face. "Unfortunately, there's a lot more to come before she's better."

He closed the file with a snap and handed it back across the counter. "Everything looks fine in here," he said briskly, "but I'll just go have a quick look at her, anyway." He started to turn away from the counter. "Oh, get Mrs.—" he slanted a quick look at Daphne "—Granger a cup of coffee, would you, please? And find her a place to sit where she won't be in anyone's way." Then he was gone, striding down the hall before either of the women could answer him.

The nurse sighed, her crossed arms all but hugging the folder to her chest. "Dr. Forrest is *so* dedicated," she said, with just exactly the inflection another woman might have used to say "*so* handsome."

"Yes, I know," Daphne murmured dryly, amused.

"Well." Peg fit the folder into its correct slot in the file and looked up at Daphne. Her smile was brisk and friendly. Her eyes were curious. "How do you like your coffee?"

"Black. But I'll get it." Daphne motioned down the hall with one hand. "I saw a machine when we came in."

"Oh, no, you don't want that. It'll dissolve your tonsils." She swung open a wooden gate at the end of the counter. "Come on around here and sit down. I'll pour you a cup of my special brew."

"You're sure I won't be in the way here?"

"Not at all." She stepped behind a chest-high partition, talking over her shoulder as she poured the coffee. "Things are a little slow this time of night. Dinner's over, visiting hours haven't really gotten started yet." She handed Daphne a cup of steaming coffee and then perched on the edge of her desk, blowing across the surface of her own cup. "Gets pretty quiet."

Daphne murmured her thanks for the coffee and took a cautious sip. Hot and strong, it burned the tip of her tongue. "What's the matter with the 'little Jenkins girl'?" she asked, more for something to say than anything else.

Hospitals, with their starchy white-clad nurses, medicinal smells, and the pain and sickness that seemed to lurk behind every door had always made her uncomfortable. She had never been in one as a patient and only seldom as a visitor, so the atmosphere was alien and vaguely anxiety-producing. She really would rather have taken Adam's suggestion and gone to his place to wait. But she had wanted to show him, indirectly at least, that she had changed at least as much as he had. And it was only going to be for a few minutes.

"She was badly burned when she pulled an electric skillet full of hot oil down on top of her," Peg said. The statement effectively reclaimed Daphne's wandering attention.

"Oh, how awful!"

"Pretty gruesome," Peg agreed. She took a sip of her coffee. "Luckily, though, it was only her legs. With physical therapy and Dr. Forrest's fine work, they should be almost as good as new in a few years."

"Adam—Dr. Forrest," Daphne corrected herself, "is doing plastic surgery on her legs?"

Peg gave her a rather censuring look. "Plastic surgery isn't only face-lifts and boob jobs," she informed Daphne somewhat sternly. "Dr. Forrest is doing a series of skin grafts on the Jenkins girl."

"Skin grafts?"

"Yes. Basically it involves taking thin strips of skin," she explained, "and applying them to the healed-over burn areas on the child's legs. Dr. Forrest did the first one yesterday afternoon."

"First one?" Daphne prompted, fascinated in spite of herself by this glimpse into Adam's world. "She'll have to have more than one operation, then?"

"Oh, yes. Several, in fact. With burns that extensive it can't all be corrected at once."

"Poor little thing."

"Peg—Oh, excuse me, I didn't know you were busy."

"That's all right, Beth." Peg put her cup down and turned to the young Oriental nurse who had come rushing up to the counter in her soundless rubber-soled shoes. "What is it?"

"Dr. Forrest wants the Chapel file. That spoiled society bit—" She glanced at Daphne and caught herself. "Mrs. Chapel claims we're ignoring her. And she wants 'the kind Dr. Forrest to check her chart' and make sure we're doing everything we should be doing." She rolled her eyes. "What she really wants is to get Dr. Forrest into her room. Preferably alone."

"Don't we all?" Peg laughed good-naturedly and handed her the file. "Anything else?"

"Well, he hasn't asked for it yet but you'd better give me the Tibbs file, too." She took the folders and tucked them securely under her arm. "Thanks, Peg," she said, dashing off down the hall.

"Looks as if he's going to be a while," Daphne commented, staring into her cup.

"He usually is." Peg picked up her coffee again. "I don't think I've ever seen Dr. Forrest get in and out of here in less than an hour and a half, even when he's only got a couple of patients to see. He always takes the time to talk a bit if they want to. Tries to cheer them. Especially the little ones."

She started to say something more but another doctor came up to the desk, requesting a patient's file, and Peg turned to find it for her. Then a teenage candy striper, her face obscured behind a vase of bright yellow marigolds, stopped to ask directions to a patient's room. Close on her heels came a young black nurse with a chart in her hands and a question in her eyes. Peg moved down to the end of the counter to confer quietly with her.

Daphne began to fidget. She had never been good at just sitting—or waiting. And having to do both, especially in a hospital, made her as antsy as a five-year-old. She wished, for a moment, that she had thought to stuff a sketch pad into her hobo bag. At least it would give her something to do while she waited.

She smiled to herself then, staring into her coffee cup as she thought of the sketches she had done this morning on the back of a paper place mat at the restaurant where Adam had taken her for breakfast.

Early as it was, they had easily found a coveted window table overlooking the Sausalito boat harbor. The sun was still struggling to break up the morning fog, spindly fingers of buttery light sparkling on the placid blue-gray water of the bay and glinting off the touches of brass on the bobbing pleasure craft. Sea gulls circled and dove, screeching stridently as they called to each other. A pelican sat patiently atop an exposed piling, waiting for handouts. But Daphne and Adam saw none of it. They had eyes only for each other.

"But where do you get your ideas?" Adam had wanted to know. He sat with his chin cupped in his hand, his elbow on the table and his eyes nowhere but on her as he waited for her answer.

"Heavens, I don't know. Nowhere. Everywhere." Daphne laughed softly, bemused by the intense expression on his face. He had never seemed to be interested—really interested—in her career before. She couldn't quite believe he was now. "They just . . . come to me, I guess."

He gave her that slow, sweet smile. "Like visions out of a dream, huh?"

"Sort of," she agreed, unconsciously echoing his posture. Elbow on the table, chin in hand, she smiled back at him. They stared at each other for a few endless seconds.

"And then what happens?" he asked.

"What happens when?"

"After these ideas just 'come to you'?"

"Then I try to get them down on paper, hopefully in my sketchbook." She continued to smile into his eyes. "But I've been known to use whatever's handy."

He pushed his plate out of the way then, the half-eaten eggs Benedict cooling as he ignored it, and flipped over the heavy paper place mat. "Show me."

"What? Right now? But I don't have any ideas right now," Daphne protested.

"Show me something you've already designed then," he urged. "I'd really like to see how a dress like you wore the other night comes into being." The blue of his eyes blazed a little brighter as they both recalled what had happened to that dress. "That was one of your designs, wasn't it?"

"Well, yes," Daphne said hesitantly, still afraid of boring him. "But..."

"Please?" he urged, looking anything but bored.

Daphne smiled and reached into her own bag to rummage for a pen. In a moment she had pushed her own breakfast away and was sketching a few of the garments from her new line of lingerie on the elongated bodies that she had learned to draw in fashion school, explaining the fabrics and colors she planned to use as she did so. Adam had seemed fascinated.

"Excuse me." A soft voice broke into her thoughts and Daphne looked up from the contemplation of her coffee cup, startled. A young woman in her mid to late twenties had approached the nurses' station. "Are you..." she began, seeing that she had Daphne's attention. "Oh, no," she said before she had even finished her question. "I can see you're not. I'm sorry. I thought for a minute that you were a nurse."

Daphne smiled and shook her head but before she could reply, Peg had already taken the situation in hand. "Mrs. Jenkins," she said, turning from the nurse she had been talking with to greet the young woman. "What good timing. Dr. Forrest has just finished going over Tiffany's chart. I'm sure he'll want to talk to you about her progress as soon as he's finished with his other patients."

"How is she?" the young woman asked timidly.

"She's doing just fine," Peg said, reaching across the counter to press Mrs. Jenkins's hand. "Why don't you go on to her room," she suggested. "I'll let Dr. Forrest know where you are as soon as he's free. Oh, wait a minute." Peg's voice stopped her as she turned in the direction of her daughter's hospital room. "Here he comes now."

Adam approached the nurses' station from the opposite direction, hurrying his steps a little as he caught sight of the young woman standing in front of the counter. He had pulled a white lab coat on over his sweater and jeans and a stethoscope hung loosely around his neck. Two metal-backed folders rested in the crook of one arm. He looked, Daphne thought, peering over the counter from her seat at one end, every inch the caring, concerned physician.

"Mrs. Jenkins," he greeted the obviously worried young mother with a brief touch on her shoulder. "I've already seen Tiffany and she's doing fine. Exactly as we expected," he told her, answering her unspoken question in a calm, assured manner. "And seeing you will make her even better."

"I have to work Saturdays," Mrs. Jenkins said apologetically, head down as if she feared his last statement had been a jab at her absence. "But my mother was here nearly all day. I—"

Adam smiled encouragingly and patted her shoulder again. "I doubt Tiffany even knew the difference," he reassured her quickly. "She slept most of the day. In fact, she had a sedative a little while ago," he warned. "So don't be alarmed if she seems a little listless to you. That's perfectly normal. Now, I still have a few things to do here." A subtle movement of his shoulder indicated the folders he carried. "But I'll stop by Tiffany's room again before I leave, to answer any questions you may have after you see her. Okay?"

"Yes, fine. Thank you, Dr. Forrest." The woman turned away and hurried down the hall to her daughter's room.

Adam dropped the folders on the counter, his eyes catching Daphne's. There was a wry twist to his lips. "I'm sorry about this," he said, dragging a hand through his hair. "But it seems like I'm going to be here a while longer than I thought."

"There's nothing to be sorry about," Daphne interjected quickly. She stood up, placing her half-empty coffee cup on the desk behind her, and came up to the counter. Peg backed away, unobtrusively busying herself at a file cabinet. "But I do think I'll take your suggestion now. About waiting for you at your place," Daphne added when he lifted an inquiring eyebrow.

"Great." Relief was evident in his tone. "That's what I came up here to talk to you about before I got sidetracked by Mrs. Jenkins." He pushed his lab coat aside as he spoke, and dug into his front pocket for his car keys. "Here." He dangled the keys over the counter, deftly capturing her hand as she reached for them to draw her down the length of the counter and through the wooden gate.

"My place is easy to find," he said, silencing her protests before she could open her mouth to suggest that she should be the one to take a taxi. "And you'll need the keys to get in, anyway." He walked her down the hall as he spoke, toward the double glass doors that led out into the parking lot. "There's a list of takeout places that deliver next to the telephone in the kitchen. Call one of them and have them deliver whatever you feel like eating at, say, eight—" he glanced at his watch "—no, better make that nine just to be on the safe side. Okay?"

Daphne tilted her head sideways and looked up at him from under her lashes. "You promise I won't end up eating alone?" The look in her eyes invited a reassuring kiss.

Adam ran the backs of two fingers down her cheek in a brief caress instead. "I promise," he said softly. Then he reached around and pulled open the door. "Go," he ordered, pushing her out. "Before I forget I have a job to do here and decide to go with you."

Daphne went, her knees still trembling from the tenderness of his gesture.

HIS HOUSE WAS EASY to find. Easy, that is, if you were a native San Franciscan which, fortunately, Daphne was. A modest-sized bungalow tucked into the maze of streets in the Russian Hill district, Adam's house had a slightly 1920s' look to it, as if it might have been built by some movie mogul as a hideaway for his lady love. The inside, however, was warm and modern and very definitely done by a 1980s' decorator.

The colors were mostly shades of brown; a tobacco-brown carpet, pale buff-colored walls that melted unobtrusively into the terra-cotta brick of the fireplace, a soft coconut-brown pit grouping scattered with plump pillows in more shades of brown and cream and a deep bittersweet orange. The orange was repeated in accent pieces around the room: a ginger-jar lamp, a tall Chinese vase by the door, an Oriental rug that stretched between the sofa and the fireplace, a dried flower arrangement on a side table.

Either Adam had become a lot more interested in decorating over the years or he had hired a decorator, Daphne thought with a smile. And, although the room accurately reflected his warmth and quiet personality, she felt sure it was the latter. Adam would never have thought to pick a color scheme that would complement his golden good looks to such advantage.

She crossed the room, tossing her bag into a corner of the sofa as she passed it, and struck a match to the fire that had already been laid in the fireplace. It blazed to life immediately, little flickers of flame dancing up around the dry eucalyptus logs, releasing their clean fresh fragrance and casting a warm glow over the room. Daphne watched it for a few minutes, delighting in the unique fragrance of the wood and the warmth of the fire on her outstretched hands.

Her stomach rumbled, reminding her that dinner had to be ordered before she could eat. Breakfast, she remembered suddenly, had only been half eaten this morning. And lunch, delicious as it was, had been sketchy: little paper cups of shrimp cocktail and individual-serving size packets of oyster crackers, eaten as they strolled along Fisherman's Wharf, with a shared banana split from the ice-cream parlor in Ghirardelli Square as dessert.

Smiling to herself, she pulled the metal fire screen closed and turned, following her nose to the kitchen and the list of takeout places that Adam had promised would be by the telephone.

A decorator had been at work in here, too, she thought, eyeing the russet squares of Mexican tile on the floor, the cream walls, the bittersweet orange counters and gleaming appliances. It looked like something from *House Beautiful*, not a thing out of place, not a single water spot marring the perfection of the double stainless steel sink.

The list was where Adam said it would be, pinned to a small corkboard next to a wall phone that was the exact shade of the cream-colored walls. Daphne pushed the bulky sleeves of her sweater up and ran the tip of her index finger down the neatly typed list. Mexican, Chinese, Greek, Italian; the selection was extensive. He must have every takeout place in San Francisco listed here, she thought wryly, wondering if he ever cooked for himself.

She called one of the Chinese restaurants on the list and then looked around for anything that might resemble a coffee maker. It was attached to the underside of one of the cupboards, a modern space-age gadget that ground the beans, brewed the coffee and kept it warm, all in less than twelve square inches of space. Now if she could only find the coffee.

Not in any of the cupboards, not in the refrigerator. The only things in there were a quart of milk, a half-eaten wheel of cheese neatly wrapped in cellophane, two apples and three one-pound bags of peanut M&Ms. She finally found a sack of gourmet coffee beans in the freezer, of all places. She started the coffee maker, guessing at the amount of beans to use, and left the kitchen to poke around the rest of the house.

The dining room echoed the color scheme of the living room, with a gleaming mahogany table surrounded by four matching chairs upholstered in cream-colored velveteen and walls papered with textured grass cloth. The guest bedroom was done in safe, nonsexist shades of bleached bone and tan, its furnishings neither masculine nor feminine in feeling. Adam's bedroom, however, was done in rich masculine shades of brown: mostly camel and milk chocolate with discreet touches of antique gold in the striped bedspread and the hardware on the traditionally styled teak furniture. The attached bathroom was all milk chocolate tile and gold towels.

And all of it—every room—was as neat and tidy and impersonal as the gleaming kitchen.

Adam had always been neat. Obsessively so, Daphne had accused more than once when they were in the midst of some argument or other. But this place went beyond neat, it looked almost as sterile as an operating room.

She wandered out of the bedroom and across the hall to the only room she hadn't yet seen. *Ah, here's where Adam lives*, she thought as she switched on the light. She hadn't realized until she saw it that what she had been looking for in the midst of this decorator's dream of a house was some sign of the man she had once been married to. She found it in Adam's den.

Oh, it had been decorated by a professional, too. The dramatic burnt umber walls and cream-colored woodwork attested to that fact. But the floor-to-ceiling bookcases were full of Adam's tattered medical books, the rolltop desk under the window held several framed family photographs, and the leather sofa sagged at one end as if that spot was where Adam habitually sat when he was reading. The long low table in front of the sofa held a brass bowl full of Adam's favorite peanut M&Ms, an untidy stack of medical journals that had spilled over onto the floor and a large book, left lying open as if Adam might have just been reading it.

Daphne moved forward, drawn by something vaguely familiar about the book on the coffee table. Only it wasn't a book, it was a photograph album. Hers and Adam's, put together when they had still been together. Until this moment she had forgotten all about it.

She sat down on the sofa, pulled her boots and socks off and curled into Adam's spot as if it were still warm from the heat of his body. She lifted the album onto her lap and began to turn the pages on what had been their life together.

There was Adam, shortly after they had first started dating, smiling at her with the wind in his golden hair and the

Bay at his back. And there they were sitting cross-legged on a blanket in Golden Gate Park with a picnic basket to one side and a half-empty bottle of cheap apple wine between them, both of them grinning like idiots at whoever was taking the picture.

And another shot of them together, heads tilted toward each other as they posed. She was looking straight into the camera, mugging for the photographer, but Adam was gazing at her, a laughing, loving expression on his face as he watched her clown.

Had he ever really looked at her like that, she wondered wistfully, running the pad of her finger over his beloved face. Would he ever look at her like that again?

She turned the page and came face-to-face with their wedding photographs. There was one large one, a big eight by ten that had been part of the package deal at the Vegas wedding chapel they had gone to. It showed them standing under an arch of white plastic flowers, a sky-blue wall at their backs.

Adam wore his only suit, a $49.99 special, purchased on sale. His tie was a three-inch-wide paisley and his hair covered his ears, but he still looked like every girl's dream of an ardent young groom. Daphne wore a simple white cotton peasant dress of her own design and making. It had a wide flounce that swooped across the bodice, baring her shoulders, a narrow yellow sash and a scalloped hem that reached to her ankles. Her long golden-brown hair hung to her waist, crowned by a wreath of daisies and baby's breath that Adam had blushingly presented to her before they left the motel.

They looked young and scared and very much in love, standing there, clutching each other's hands as they stared solemnly into the camera.

The other wedding pictures were snapshots, taken mostly by Sunny or Brian, who had come with them so they wouldn't have to have strangers act as witnesses. There was Daphne and Sunny, bride and bride's attendant. And Adam and Brian, groom and best man. And Sunny and Brian, clowning as he pretended to drag an unwilling substitute bride to the altar. And then Daphne and Adam again, "kissing the bride" a second time in front of the garish wedding chapel for the benefit of a photographer who had been blubbering into her handkerchief the first time.

They had been so much in love. So much.

When had love ceased to be enough?

Daphne sniffled a bit, wiping at her damp eyes as the bittersweet memories assailed her. She continued turning the pages.

Maybe this is where it started, she thought, coming to stop on the page that held a faded newspaper clipping. "Radical feminist assaults cameraman," the caption read under a grainy photograph of a long-haired, jean-clad Daphne allegedly trying to knock a cameraman unconscious with her homemade placard. As someone had said at Sunny's party, Adam had been mad enough to bust a gut.

"What the hell did you think you were doing, marching down Market Street with a bunch of harebrained man-haters?" Adam had raged, steam practically coming from his ears as he paced their small apartment. "Just what were you trying to prove?"

"Feminists do not hate men," she had pointed out, struggling to hide her tears. Tears that were a result of both Adam's anger and the unsettling experience of being arrested. "At least, not in general," she had added ominously. "And we were trying to prove that women have rights, too."

"By trying to brain a cameraman? Dammit, Daffy, you're my wife! Why can't you act like it?"

"Act like what? Your mother?" she shot back. His mother was a loving, tradition-bound woman who thought wives had been put on this earth to cater to their husbands and sons. Too enraged to think before she spoke, Daphne forgot that Adam couldn't really be blamed for having absorbed some of her old-fashioned ideas. She forgot, too, that he was trying to overcome them. "Cooking and cleaning and bowing down before the great doctor-to-be? With no opinions of my own. Is that the kind of wife you want? A little robot woman?"

"Dammit, Daffy, you know that's not what I meant. I was afraid you'd be hurt. You *could* have been hurt, you know! Besides, what's wrong with being like my mother?"

The argument, Daphne remembered, had finally ended up like all their other arguments. In bed, with ardent exclamations of love and regret and forgiveness—and no real solution.

The click of the front door brought her head up. The sound of footsteps muffled in the plush carpet had her eyes seeking the brass clock on the opposite wall. Eight-thirty. Adam was home earlier than he had planned, she thought, feeling a surge of joy shoot through her. Daphne uncurled her feet and leaned forward to place the album back on the coffee table. A voice froze her in the act of rising from the sofa.

"Adam?" The light feminine voice lifted in inquiry. "Where are you?"

Daphne melted back into the corner of the sofa. Some woman obviously had a key to Adam's house. A picture of the dark-haired nurse, Ginny, flashed into her mind. Would Adam give his house key to a woman who was only a friend? A woman who was, as he had said, not part of a "couple"?

"Adam, it's me." There was a light knock on the half-closed door to the den and Adam's sister stepped into the room. "I just stopped by to pick up that textbook on organic chemistry for my..." Her voice trailed off as she caught sight of Daphne. Her blue eyes widened. "You!" she breathed, incredulous. "What are you doing here?"

Startled, Daphne told her the literal truth. "Waiting for Adam."

Marcia advanced into the middle of the room, her eyes narrowing suspiciously. "How did you get in?"

Daphne's eyebrows rose. She knew Marcia didn't like her and she thought she knew why, but that was no reason for her to speak as if she suspected Daphne of breaking and entering. "With a key."

"You mean Adam gave you a key?" Marcia said the words as if she could hardly believe them.

"Obviously."

Marcia glared at her. "I don't believe it," she stated emphatically.

"No?" Daphne shrugged, fighting the quick rise of animosity she felt toward Adam's sister. "Well, then, I guess you'll just have to wait until Adam comes home and ask him, won't you?" She glanced up at the clock again. "He should be coming in anytime now," she offered. "We're supposed to eat at nine."

Marcia sank down into the straight-backed chair in front of the rolltop desk. "But his car's in the driveway."

"Yes, I know. I drove it back from the hospital. Adam's going to take a taxi." Daphne stood. "I made some coffee when I came in. Would you like a cup?"

Marcia didn't seem to have heard her. "I can't believe he'd actually see you again. You!" she said scathingly, as if

Daphne were some lower form of life. Her eyes pinned Daphne to where she stood, something very close to hate in their blue depths.

"Why not?" Daphne asked, hardly able to comprehend how such an emotion could be directed at her by someone she barely knew.

"Because you divorced him!"

"Adam divorced me," Daphne said, her voice gone quite cold.

"After you deserted him!"

Anger—and pain—flashed in Daphne's eyes for a moment. "You've got your facts slightly wrong," she informed Marcia coolly. "Desertion had noth—"

"You left him to go to New York," Marcia interrupted. "To be a *fashion designer*." She injected the last two words with as much scorn as possible. "And you didn't come back."

Because I wasn't wanted back, Daphne thought, but said nothing in her own defense. Let Marcia think what she liked. It seemed she would anyway, no matter what Daphne said. "I'm going into the kitchen for that cup of coffee." She paused in the doorway. "You're welcome to join me." She left the room without a backward glance.

The smell of fresh, too strong coffee permeated the small spotless kitchen. Daphne found a glazed earthenware mug in one of the cupboards and poured herself a full cup. Her hands shook.

Why would Marcia have such a warped view of what had happened? True, she had only been thirteen at the time of the divorce, and girls of that age tended to be fanciful, especially if they were half in love with their oldest brother. But still, the only way she could have gotten everything so backward was if someone had told it to her that way. And that someone could have only been Adam. But why would

Adam have made her out to be the heavy when *he* was the one who had filed for divorce?

A sharp rat-a-tat-tat interrupted her thoughts and Daphne jumped. She set the cup of unwanted coffee on the counter and hurried toward the front door. It opened before she got there and Adam, one arm cradling a sack of steaming food, hurried in out of the foggy night air.

"Great timing, huh?" he said, grinning as he pushed the door shut with his shoulder. "I intercepted the delivery boy at the door." He sniffed appreciatively. "Hmm, Chinese. My favorite." He entered the kitchen, dropping the sack on the counter, and turned to take Daphne into his arms. She avoided his embrace. His face clouded instantly, the happy grin gone. "Daffy, what's wrong?"

"Nothing," she lied, motioning toward the hall with one hand. "Marcia's here."

"So?" He reached for her again. "I'll say hello to her in a minute." He lifted her chin with a forefinger. "Right now I want to say hello to you." He smiled down into her eyes. "Hello, Daffy," he said softly, placing a gentle kiss on her lips.

Daphne couldn't help it, she kissed him back. For a moment, seconds only, they were lost in the first sweet, tender touch of mouth on mouth. Then Adam's arms tightened, lifting her, and Daphne arched up to meet him.

"Hello, Adam," Marcia said from behind them, her voice disapproving.

Adam lifted his head, and self-consciously his arms dropped from around Daphne. Apparently, being caught with his arms around his ex-wife made him uncomfortable, she thought. "Marcia. I didn't know you intended to come by tonight."

"Obviously." The words dripped sarcasm. She leaned against the doorjamb, arms folded across her chest. "What's she doing here?" She indicated Daphne with a contemptuous toss of her blond head.

Adam frowned a warning. "Daffy's my guest."

"Why?"

"I don't think I care for the tone of your voice, young lady."

"Oh, for crying out loud. Don't go all big brother on me, Adam," Marcia snapped.

"Then don't act like a baby sister."

"But that's just it. I *am* your sister." She moved into the kitchen, completely ignoring Daphne, and put her hand on Adam's arm, her blue eyes wide as she gazed intently up into his face. "And I'm worried about you."

"There's nothing for you to worry about," he said gently.

"There is, too. And you know it!" She flashed a venomous look at Daphne. "She almost ruined your life once," Marcia said passionately. "And she'll do it again if you let her."

Adam's big hand came down on Marcia's, silencing her as he pressed it to his forearm. "You haven't got the faintest idea what you're talking about, Marcia," he said quietly. "You were only thirteen when Daffy and I got divorced. Hardly old enough to understand everything that was going on." He snorted. "Hell, I barely understood it myself."

"But, Adam—"

"No buts." Adam stopped her with a shake of his head. "I don't want to hear any more about it."

"But I'm worried about you!"

"I know." He patted her hand and put her away from him. "But I'm a big boy now, quite capable of handling my own affairs."

"Is that why she's here?" Marcia spat, her eyes raking over Daphne's slender form as she pressed back against a counter for support. "For some tacky little affair?"

"That's enough!" Adam's voice cracked through the room like a whip, all gentleness gone. "Not one more word," he said when she opened her mouth. "Not another word. In fact, I'd appreciate it if you'd go on home before you say anything else you're going to regret."

Marcia stood where she was, looking stubborn.

"*Now*, Marcia."

With one last venomous look at Daphne, jaw clenched against the words Adam had forbidden her to say, Marcia fled. The door banged behind her, shaking some of the paintings on the living room wall.

The silence was deafening.

9

"SHE'S RIGHT, YOU KNOW," Daphne said after a minute, her voice small and defeated. "I am here for a tacky little affair."

"That's not true!" Adam said tightly.

"It is," she insisted, too miserable herself to be surprised at the vehemence of his denial. "I came to Sunny's party—I'm here now—with the express intent of having an affair with you. If that's not tacky, then I don't know what is." She flashed him a quick, guilty look. "Marcia was right."

"Marcia doesn't know what the hell she's talking about." He came across the kitchen in one long stride and grabbed her by the shoulders. "And, obviously, neither do you."

Daphne winced at the tone of his voice. "Are we going to fight now?" she said, head down as she stared at his sweatered chest.

"I don't know." He gave her a quizzical look, bending his knees a bit to peer into her face. "Will we end up in bed if we do?" he asked hopefully.

Daphne gave a resigned sigh. "Probably."

His hands slipped from her shoulders to her back, drawing her against his chest. "All right," he said agreeably. "Then let's fight. Who starts?"

"Oh, Adam." She gave a helpless little half laugh into his chest. "This is serious."

"Of course it is." He nuzzled the soft golden-brown curls at her temple. "Because I'm going to go crazy if I don't make love to you soon," he breathed against her ear. "Very soon."

"Oh, Adam," she said again, fighting the urge to melt into his arms as she wanted to. She brought her hands up between their bodies, intending to put some space between them. They rested against his chest instead. "Don't try to charm me, please," she pleaded. "It isn't fair."

"All's fair in love and war." His lips moved against the curve of her jaw as he spoke.

"And which is this?"

Adam's mouth went very still against her flesh. "I don't know," he said, lifting his head to look into her eyes. All playfulness was gone from his expression. "You tell me."

"I don't know, either," she wailed, pulling out of his arms. She turned her back on him, fooling with the untasted cup of coffee that sat cooling on the counter. "I thought it would be so, oh, I don't know—" her shoulders lifted under the bulky butterscotch sweater "—easy, I guess. I'd come out here. We'd have a torrid affair, get thoroughly sick of each other and then I could go back to New York and get on with my life but..."

"But?" Adam prompted, his voice whisper soft behind her. She could feel the tip of his finger touching her hair, lightly tracing the downward curve of her skull.

"But I find that I can't have an affair as easily as that. Not casually, with no expectations and no hopes for the future. Not...not with you."

His hand dropped. "Why not with me?"

"Because I was married to you, Adam. Because I loved you once, with all the...the passion of a young girl. And those old feelings keep getting tangled up with what I'm feeling now so that I don't really know *what* I'm feeling." She turned to face him, eyes wide and misted with unshed tears as she gazed up at him, seeking understanding. "Does that make any sense at all?"

"Oh, yes," he breathed. He put his arms around her, as gently as if she were a child, one big hand cupping the back of her head, and laid his cheek against her hair. "Perfect sense."

Daphne sighed and let him hold her, accepting the comfort he offered. "I know the passion's still there," she said, her face hidden against his chest. "There's never been any doubt about that. You've always been able to arouse me without half trying," she admitted. "But I don't know if that's all it is. I mean, there *is* something else, something more, but I don't know if it's real or just a memory of what I used to feel." She shivered in his arms and he pulled her closer. "I want you, Adam, but I'm afraid."

"I know," he murmured. "So am I."

Daphne lifted her head, tilting it back against his hand to look up into his face. "You? Of what?"

"Of the same things you are, Daffy. Of you and what you can make me feel." His other hand came up to caress her cheek, tenderly brushing the soft strands of hair back from her face as he struggled to find the words to express what he needed to say. "You've always been able to arouse such... such *intense* emotions in me. Been able to stir me up so that half the time I didn't know if I was coming or going." He caught her eyes and held them. "The only thing I was always completely sure of was that I wanted you... and that you wanted me."

"But it isn't enough, is it?" she said miserably. "Not then and not now."

"Not then, no," Adam agreed. "But we were young and impatient and too stupid to realize a good thing when we had it. We didn't have enough experience to know that you had to work at making it even better. At making it last."

"And now?" Daphne whispered, her hands unconsciously curling into the fabric of his sweater as she waited for his answer.

"And now?" Adam sighed heavily. "Now, I don't know. It could be good again, I think. There's something special between us," he said slowly, carefully, his eyes touching each feature of her upturned face. "Something—" he struggled for a word "—rare, even. Something inside me, here—" he touched his chest "—that calls to something in you. But I don't know what's going to happen any more than you do. I don't know if it's enough. We'll just have to wait and see. In the meantime..." His voice trailed off as he brushed the pad of his thumb across the tender curve of her bottom lip.

"In the meantime?" Daphne prompted breathlessly, her lips pursed in an almost-kiss against his thumb.

"In the meantime, we get to know each other."

"Meaning?"

"Meaning we spend more days like today, just being together. Meaning we have dinner here tonight. We relax. We talk. And, maybe, if it feels right, if we both want it, we make love. Just like any other healthy single adults who find themselves attracted to each other."

"And when I go back to New York?"

"I'll call you," he said simply. "Maybe you'll even call me." He smiled suddenly. "That is, if you're still a liberated woman?"

Daphne smiled back. "Always."

"Good." He bent his head then, lifting her mouth to his with the hand cupped at the back of her head, and kissed her softly, with exquisite gentleness. "Now, are you ready for the first step?"

"Hmm." Daphne murmured dreamily, wanting the kiss to go on forever.

"Dinner?" he reminded her, his mouth against hers.

"Uh-huh, whenever you are."

He kissed her once more, quickly, as if he were afraid that a more lengthy caress would be unwise, and put her away from him. He turned to the bag on the counter and opened it. "Plates are in that cupboard," he said gruffly, gesturing over his shoulder as he pulled several cartons out of the bag. "Silver in the top drawer by the stove." He stooped, pulling a large tray out of a lower cupboard. "Put them on this," he instructed. "We'll eat in the living room in front of the fire."

"Do you want coffee?"

He picked up the cup on the counter, tasting it. "Not this stuff," he said, grimacing at her as he put it down. "Tastes strong enough to remove paint. How 'bout some wine instead?"

"Lovely," Daphne agreed, following him into the living room.

He put the tray down on the Oriental carpet in front of the fireplace, motioning her to sit down while he moved to the mirrored wet bar tucked into a corner of the large room. Dropping to his haunches, he opened a cabinet beneath it and flicked on the tape deck. The muted sound of a single jazz saxophone filled the silences between the crackle and hiss of the fire. A cork popped softly, glasses tinkled against each other as he lifted them from the shelf, and then he was back beside her, sinking down into a cross-legged position on the opposite side of the tray.

"A nice, dry Riesling," he commented, handing her a delicate tulip-shaped glass of the shimmering liquid. Daphne accepted it with a smile, holding it up as he raised his glass for a toast. "Here's to getting to know each other again."

Their glasses touched, eyes meeting over the rim.

"To getting to know each other again," Daphne echoed softly. She lifted the glass to her lips and drank deeply, her eyes never leaving his.

"So, what would you like?" she asked, setting her glass on the hearth. She pushed up the sleeves of her sweater and picked up a plate, gesturing toward the cartons on the tray. "Sweet and sour shrimp? Almond chicken? Beef strips with snow peas? Fried rice?"

"Everything, please." He leaned back against the edge of the sofa, legs extended, ankles crossed, watching her as she put a little of everything on his plate. "You look beautiful in the firelight," he said suddenly.

Daphne looked up, startled, the laden plate extended midway between them as she paused in the act of passing it to him.

"Why so surprised?" He put his wineglass on the tray and reached out to take the plate from her. "Surely you've been told that before."

"Not by you."

He shook his head. "By me," he said positively. "Hundreds of times."

"Only. . ." Incredibly, she felt herself beginning to blush. Head averted, she handed him a fork. "Only in bed," she finished softly.

He caught at her fingers, holding them when she would have drawn her hand back. "Only in bed?" He seemed dumbfounded. "Really?"

Daphne nodded. "Really."

Adam swore softly. "What a stupid young fool I must have been." He came away from the sofa, leaning forward as he brought her hand to his lips. "Forgive me."

"Don't be silly, Adam." Gently, she pulled her fingers from him and began filling her own plate. "There's nothing to forgive."

"Come over here," he said when she had made her selections, patting the space next to him. "Please."

Daphne came, scooting around the tray so she could lean back against the sofa. They ate without speaking for a few long minutes, nothing but the gentle hiss and crackle of the fire, the low wail of the saxophone, and the sound of forks against china breaking the silence.

"When do you have to go back to New York?"

"My return ticket says Wednesday morning."

"And what do you say?"

Daphne pushed the food around on her plate. "Wednesday morning. I *do* have a business to run, Adam," she began, anticipating an objection. "It doesn't run itself."

"Did I say it did? No, don't answer that," he said before she could. "I implied it. I'm sorry. I know what you do for a living is as important to you as what I do is to me."

Daphne turned her head, eyes wide as she raised them to his face.

"Surprised you, didn't I?" He grinned disarmingly.

"Yes," she admitted. "You did." She paused, looking down at her plate for a moment. "You're full of surprises."

"Am I?"

"Definitely."

"Well." He shifted uneasily. "I guess I've learned a few things in the last eleven years." He pushed the food around on his plate, not looking at her. "Things that would have saved me a lot of trouble if I'd learned them years ago."

"Such as?"

"Such as women are entitled to a life outside of marriage," he said gruffly, with the air of a man who had something to say and was going to say it, no matter what. "Such as no one wants to live with a stiff-necked, pompous jackass who thinks his way is the only way."

"You?" Daphne asked, her eyes round.

Adam nodded, a faint blush beginning to color his beard-roughened cheeks. Talking about himself, baring his soul, had always made Adam as uncomfortable as a frog in a biology lab. Daphne couldn't help teasing him just a little.

"Well-l-l," she said, head tilted as she considered him from under the sweep of her lashes. "I'll go along with the stiff-necked part. And you certainly could be pompous at times, especially when you were talking about the sanctity of the medical profession. But jackass? I don't know." She pursed her lips thoughtfully. "No," she said finally, shaking her head. "I never thought you were a jackass." She paused, waiting until he looked at her. "Not *all* the time, anyway."

He forked up a bit of fried rice before answering. "In that case," he said, hiding a smile, "I guess we won't go into what a jackass you could be at times."

"No," Daphne agreed with a heartfelt sigh. "Let's not." She took a tiny bit of chicken. "I'll be back in San Francisco before the end of the month," she said then, reverting back to the topic that was on both their minds. "Trunk shows for my summer line."

"What's a trunk show?"

"Just an informal sort of fashion show at the stores that carry my line. Lets the end customer, the consumer, meet the designer in person and get a close look at the clothes."

"Will you be here long?"

"A week or so."

There was a small, intense silence.

"Will you stay with me?"

Daphne put her picked-over plate down on the tray and reached for her wine. "Here?"

"Yes, here." He shot her a sideways glance. "Where else would you stay with me?"

Daphne didn't answer that. "Yes," she said, answering his previous question instead.

There was another small silence. Adam continued eating. Daphne sipped her wine.

"What about Marcia?" she asked, after a moment.

"What about her?"

"She won't like it."

"No, probably not. But Marcia hasn't got anything to do with us." Adam put his empty plate on top of hers on the tray. "And I don't intend to ask her permission, so it hardly matters."

Daphne took a sip of her wine. "Doesn't it? Matter, I mean." She drew her long legs under her, her shoulder against the sofa as she turned to look up at him. "You've always been close to your family and I'd hate to cause trouble—Adam?" she said, but Adam wasn't listening. He was staring at her with a bemused expression on his face.

"You really are incredibly beautiful in the firelight." He took her wineglass from her hand and put it on the tray, pushing the whole thing out of the way without taking his eyes from her face. "It makes your skin glow like peach silk," he murmured, touching her cheek with his fingertips. "And brings out the gold in your hair."

Daphne became very, very still. Waiting.

His fingers feathered through the wispy curls on her forehead. "It's so soft. Like a baby's curls." He tucked a bit of hair behind her ear with the tip of one finger. "And you have such little ears. I don't think I ever noticed what perfect little ears you have," he said, tilting her head sideways to take a better look. He leaned forward and ran his tongue around the curved rim of her ear.

Daphne gasped softly and stopped breathing.

"I think I like your hair this way," Adam continued, his right hand sliding down the side of her neck as he spoke, burrowing under the collar of her bulky sweater. His thumb rested in the soft hollow at the front of her throat, his fingers splayed along the tiny bones in the back of her neck. He pressed his lips to the warm flesh just under the opposite ear.

Daphne's head fell against his hand, baring her neck, offering, asking for more.

"It gives me access to all sorts of areas that I never noticed before. Your little ears. Your neck. You have a beautiful neck. Very elegant." He nuzzled his face against her neck for a moment, placing soft open-mouthed kisses all down its length, and then drew back to look at her. "You're an altogether elegant woman, Daffy. I like the way you've grown up."

"I like the way you've grown up, too," she said, her voice no more than a husky whisper. "I thought so the minute I saw you sitting out in the audience at the fashion show." She lifted her hand slowly and laid it against his cheek.

"What did you think?" he asked eagerly, turning into her palm, holding it against his lips with his left hand.

Her fingers curled against his mouth, soft as a flower curling against the night. "I thought you looked experienced and knowing and devastatingly sexy," she admitted, her eyes turning to pools of liquid gold as she watched the heat building in his. "I thought you had developed an infinitely more interesting face. And that you had..." She paused, inhaling sharply as he pulled her palm away from his mouth and began to kiss the end of each slender finger, touching the spaces between them with the tip of his tongue.

"That I had what? Go on," he urged gruffly.

"That you had kept the—ah, Adam!" His lips had found their way to the sensitive skin on the inside of her wrist. "You had kept the magnificent physique that first attracted me to you."

"Is that what first attracted you to me?" he said. His voice was lazy, almost slurred, but his eyes were hot and hungry. "My body?"

"Umm." She swayed toward him a little. Her lips were parted, wanting. Her breasts were swollen and aching beneath the bulky butterscotch sweater. "At first."

"That's what attracted me to you, too, at first. Your body." He rubbed his cheek against the inside of her forearm where the flesh was pale, the skin transparent enough to show the faint blue tracery of her veins. "When I looked up—flat on my back on the sidewalk—and saw those long silky legs straddling that bike... I wanted them to be straddling me."

"Oh, God, Adam, kiss me!"

Slowly, agonizingly slowly, Adam's right hand tightened on the back of her neck, drawing her toward him. He kissed her softly, gently, all the fierce, raging needs firmly under control. He nibbled, teasing her with quick open-mouthed kisses. Greedy, needing, Daphne strained forward, trying to increase the maddening butterfly pressure of his mouth on hers.

Adam drew back, thwarting her. "No," he murmured, gently stroking the back of her neck with the pads of all four fingers. His eyes were heavy-lidded, simmering like a blue flame deliberately held on low. "Remember what I said this morning? Slowly this time. Very slowly."

Daphne struggled to understand, but the husky intensity of his voice, the seething passion in his eyes, were as drugging as a narcotic.

"I want to savor every—" he came to his knees, tilting her head back as he took its weight in his palm, and touched his lips to the rounded point of her chin "—delectable—" his mouth descended to the long elegant column of her throat, the tip of his tongue tracing a wet line down her windpipe

"—inch." He nuzzled his face into the collar of her sweater and placed his mouth over the soft hollow at the base of her throat, sucking gently.

Daphne sighed brokenly, and her hands fluttered up and down his hard ribs, seeking to draw him closer.

Adam lifted his head and looked deeply into her eyes. "I want to make love with you, Daphne," he said hoarsely, his voice thick with passion, his hands trembling as they held her head. His soft words were half statement, half question.

"I want to make love with you, too," Daphne answered without a moment's hesitation.

He stood, pulling her to her feet, and led her toward the bedroom. It seemed cool after the heat in front of the fireplace. Cool and quiet and dark.

"Don't move. Don't do anything until I get back," Adam said, standing her beside the big bed.

Daphne stood there docilely, listening to the sounds of him moving around in the darkness. She heard the slide of his shoes as he took them off, the muted thump as they landed on the carpeted floor. She smelled the sharp sulfur fragrance of a match as he lit the cluster of fat ivory candles on the dresser, and then the softer, sweeter scent of sandlewood as they burned. She saw the crisp dark brown of the sheets as he pulled the striped bedspread off of the bed and peeled back the blankets. They were piped in cream, Daphne noticed, and the pillowcases were cream piped in brown.

He came around the bed then, without her quite being aware that he had moved. He reached for the buckle of her belt and released the catch. It fell to the floor with a dull thud. Like a child, Daphne raised her arms, waiting for him to pull the sweater off over her head. It joined the belt on the floor. He unbuttoned her leather pants and lowered the zipper, then knelt to peel them down her legs. Daphne placed her hands on his shoulders, balancing herself as she lifted each foot to step out of her pants.

Adam pushed them out of the way and rose, his hands whispering over the curves of her body as he straightened, feathering lightly over the smoothness of her bare calves and thighs, her rounded hips, the inward slope of her waist, the swell of her breasts under the peach teddy.

Daphne shivered at the feather-light touch, little ripples of desire dancing madly over her flesh. She reached for the hem of his sweater.

"Not yet," Adam whispered hoarsely.

Daphne's hands fell back to her sides, waiting.

He placed his palms on her shoulders, rubbing lightly as if reacquainting himself with the satiny texture of her skin. Then he hooked a finger under the narrow straps of the teddy and eased them down, one at a time. He kissed one bare shoulder, then the other, and pulled the straps a little further down her arms. The silky fabric slid a bit lower and then clung, revealing all but the hardened tips of her breasts. Adam paused again and bent his head, brushing lips softly over the upper curves of her breasts, planting moist baby kisses on the random freckles.

Daphne moaned, head back, hands clenched at her sides as her body lifted to him with a will of its own.

Adam stilled, his fingers tightening on the straps, his lips pressed against the warm slope of her breast, as if he were taking a moment to catch his breath. Then he lifted his head and pulled the straps the rest of the way down so that they dangled past her clenched hands, baring her to the waist.

His eyes widened, the tightly leashed control slipping a notch as he took in the sheer perfection of her high proud breasts with their puckered cocoa-brown nipples, the narrow, fragile-looking rib cage, the narrower waist.

"You're so beautiful," he breathed after a minute. His fingers feathered over her chest, skimming lightly past the thrusting breasts to clasp her slim waist, measuring it in his trembling hands. "You're smaller than I remember. More fragile." His hands smoothed back up her rib cage. "Except here." He cupped her breasts from the underside, plumping them up as he weighed their fullness in his palms. Then he bent his head swiftly, as if he could wait no longer, and took one pebbled nipple between his lips. Holding it gently, he rolled it between his teeth as his tongue flicked across the tip.

Daphne whimpered and swayed toward him, her body gone liquid with desire. Her arms came up, circling his neck, and her hands curled into his golden hair to hold him even closer to her hungering breasts.

Adam's arms went around her waist, sustaining her. A moment later, one hand cupped the back of her head, and she felt herself begin to fall backward, supported in Adam's arms as he lowered her to the bed.

He came down beside her, balanced on one elbow as he buried his face in the lavishness of her breasts. He nibbled on the creamy ivory flesh, tasting, licking, savoring them as he had her lips. He ran his tongue from the freckled upper slopes to the soft plumpness at the sides, along the sweet vulnerable curve underneath and back up again, teasing them to aching hardness.

One big hand still tenderly cupped the back of her head, making Daphne feel fragile and precious and adored. His other hand lay on her stomach, the tips of his fingers rubbing lightly, hypnotically, over the slippery fabric of her peach teddy just above her mound. *That* hand made her feel wild and wanton and hungry for more—much more.

She moved restlessly on the bed, one knee lifting as she turned toward him. Her hands loosened their death grip on his hair, shifting, urging his mouth to her turgid, aching nipple. He resisted her efforts at direction, turning his head instead to kiss the soft pale flesh of her inner arm.

"Not yet," he murmured again, maddeningly. "I want to savor you this time. Taste you." He nipped her arm lightly and then laved it with his tongue. "I want to touch you all over." The hand on her stomach moved, circling, so that his fingertips just brushed over the silk covered triangle at the apex of her thighs. "I want you wild with need," he whispered huskily. "Wild with want."

Daphne arched reflexively, her body seeking a firmer touch, a more intimate caress. "I *am* wild."

"Not as wild as you're going to be," he promised solemnly and lowered his head to her breasts again.

He circled her right nipple slowly, with just the tip of his tongue, wetting her skin with his moist hot breath, making her ache for him to take it into his mouth. When he did, she arched high, stiffening for a moment at the sharp searing pleasure that ripped through her.

His free hand feathered up her stomach at the same time, doubling the pleasure as he captured the other nipple and gently, skillfully, rolled it between thumb and forefinger.

Daphne sighed, warmth spreading through her like hot honey, and her spine floated back down to settle against the bed. Her hands dropped to his shoulders and rested there, softly, like fallen flower petals against the grass, quiescent under the drugging ministrations of his mouth and hand. She felt liquid, weightless; as if she could lie there forever, content merely to have him touching and suckling at her breasts while she floated on the warm waves of sensation that rolled over her body like swells on the surface of the sea.

But then his hand slid back down her stomach and slipped under the edge of the silky peach material that was bunched around her hips. He cupped her warmth and moistness in his palm, the heel of his hand pressing down, rotating, two fingers pressing inward, unerringly finding her most sensitive secret places.

Daphne's body surged upward, her fingers curling into the fabric of his sweater, and she uttered a strangled little sound that was half a cry of ecstasy, half his name. Adam shifted, moving upward to capture her cries with his lips. He thrust his tongue into her mouth: swirling, probing, tasting, giving, taking, mimicking the movements of his fingers in her body.

The swells of pleasure became waves, huge waves, building strength and speed and power as they raced toward the shore, tumbling Daphne over and over in their wake. She couldn't stop them, didn't want to stop them, would drown if they didn't stop soon...

Her body tightened spasmodically, arching as she crested a climax of feeling that hit her like a tidal wave. Her legs crossed, trapping his hand between her thighs. Her hands clenched in his sweater, holding and pushing at the same time. She tore her mouth away from his. "Take it off," she demanded hoarsely, drinking in great gulps of air. "I'm wild now, Adam," she panted. "Wild with wanting you. Please, take your clothes off and love me. Now!"

"Not yet." He repeated that same maddening phrase like a litany. His voice was thick with passion, wild with a wanting of his own as he evaded her clutching hands and slid down her body. "Not yet, sweet baby," he breathed against the quivering skin of her body. "I haven't tasted all of you yet."

10

"UH-HUH. YES, GOT IT." Daphne sat in one of Adam's velveteen, padded dining room chairs, her bare feet propped up on another one, rapidly making notes on a lined yellow pad as she listened to the voice on the other end of the phone.

Adam's invitation to stay with him during her next trip to San Francisco had turned into almost six weeks of conducting her business on a transcontinental basis. She was getting very good at it.

"Yes, the sketches arrived in perfect condition. No problems. Umm-hmm. Well, I don't think so but maybe you'd better double-check that."

She pushed a huge, short-haired marmalade cat off her notepad and then relented and idly scratched him behind the ears as she continued her part of the conversation.

"And the shelter people were pleased with the fund raiser?" she said after a minute. "That's great, Elaine. You did a fine job," she congratulated her assistant warmly. "I'm so pleased with the way you're taking charge of things."

She paused for a moment, listening. "This coming Monday," she answered, glancing at the open appointment book spread out on the table. "Flight 487...no, I'll take a taxi...plenty of time," she said airily. "Mr. Chan isn't due until Wednesday. Surely you can hold the fort alone for three more days, can't you?" She smiled to herself, amused. "Yes, I thought so."

The cat jumped off the table, bored with his mistress's halfhearted attention, and stalked away.

"Oh, and one more thing, Elaine. Tell Hiram—" Hiram was her lawyer "—that I'm sending him a copy of a partnership agreement I'd like him to look over for me."

"A partnership agreement?" Elaine said carefully.

"Uh-huh." Daphne smiled at the gray Persian who sat on the opposite end of the table cleaning herself, and then dropped her bomb into the conversation. It was something she had been intending to do for months; Elaine was more ready for the responsibility—and the reward. "It's about time I gave you a piece of the action, don't you think?"

"A piece of the . . ." Elaine's voice rose to a squeak. "You mean you're making me a partner?"

"Not a *full* partner," Daphne warned, pleased that her little surprise had come off so well. "Just twenty percent to start and—"

"Twenty percent! Of Night Lights?"

Daphne chuckled. "What else have I got twenty percent of to give away? Not that I'm *giving* it away, anyway. You've earned it."

"Oh, Daphne, I don't know what to say. I—"

"Well, don't say anything," Daphne advised. "I haven't got time to listen to you. Sunny'll be here any minute and I've got to get some of this mess straightened up before I leave or Mrs. Drecker will have a fit."

"Who?"

"Adam's housekeeper." Daphne shuddered. "A real neatness freak. She actually moves the furniture when she vacuums."

Elaine laughed. "Lucky for you."

"Don't I know it." Daphne grinned into the receiver. "Be sure to tell Hiram to explain the agreement to you, okay? Gotta go." She hung up before Elaine could say another word.

"Go on, Queenie," she said to the gray cat, shooing it off the table. "Go find someplace else to take your bath. You're in my way."

Quickly, she straightened the sketches and notepads spread out across Adam's dining room table, sorting them into haphazard piles according to size. She gathered up her coloring pencils with a swoop of one hand, dropping them into the earthenware mug that served as a pencil cup and then leaned down, blowing eraser crumbs off the smooth mahogany surface, not even noticing that they fluttered to the tobacco carpet.

"There," she said, smacking her palms together as if to dust them off.

She picked up a coffee mug and a plate smeared with the dried remains of her breakfast and carried them out to the kitchen, adroitly stepping over the telephone extension cord, which stretched from the corner of the dining room table, across the floor, and down the hall to Adam's den. Leaving the dishes in the sink for Mrs. Drecker to do when she came in, Daphne hurried back down the hall to the bedroom.

No longer excessively tidy and impersonal—except after Mrs. Drecker had just left—the bedroom definitely looked lived in. A satin mule lay halfway between the bathroom and closet doors, a pale yellow teddy lay in a crumpled heap under the bedside table next to a pair of black silk briefs. A bright salmon-pink scarf trailed from a half-open dresser drawer and three cats sprawled across the middle of the unmade king-sized bed.

Daphne claimed long-term kinship with two of them; Queenie, the aloof gray Persian, and Mack, the fat orange marmalade so named because of his resemblance to a truck, were strays that had taken up residence in her New York apartment years ago. She had brought them with her on her last bi-coastal trip at Adam's urging because Elaine, who had been taking care of them during Daphne's increasingly lengthy absences from the Big Apple, was allergic. It had taken them less than a week to settle into Adam's house, and now they treated it as their own.

The third drowsing feline was a half-grown kitten, christened Tiger for obvious reasons, who had wandered up the front walk one foggy San Francisco night not too many days ago, begging for food. He had been fed and offered shelter for the night and, knowing a good thing when he saw it, had decided to stay.

"Don't bother to get up, guys," Daphne said, passing by the bed on her way to the closet.

Tiger slit one green eye open, yawned, and went back to sleep. The other two didn't even move.

Daphne rummaged around in the closet, shifting through the "few clothes" that were taking up more and more of Adam's rack space as she tried to find something that would be appropriate for both office hunting and a protest march. Nothing seemed quite right.

She finally settled on a pair of pleated-front, straight-legged camel slacks, a loose ivory silk shirt with the collar turned up against her neck and a camel Shaker sweater tied over her shoulders in case the May weather turned breezy, as it was wont to do on the slightest provocation. She was just stepping into a pair of low heeled tan-and-brown spectator pumps when the doorbell rang.

"Ah, Mrs. Drecker. Finally," she muttered, trying to thread a slim tan leather belt through the loops on her slacks as she hurried toward the front door. The belt loops weren't cooperating. She came to a stop in the hallway and twisted around, trying to see what the problem was. The doorbell rang again. "I'm coming, Mrs. Drecker," she hollered as she fumbled with the belt. "Wait just a second."

And wait Mrs. Drecker would, even if it took Daphne ten minutes to get to the door. The housekeeper had her own key but she had refused to use it ever since the Friday morning when she had walked in on Adam and Daphne fixing a late breakfast—and wearing only one towel between them. Daphne couldn't help smiling as she remembered the scene.

Adam had been standing at the kitchen counter, playing cooking school instructor as he demonstrated the proper way to make a pot of coffee. Daphne, in sole possession of the towel, was making toast. Neither of them had heard the front door open—Adam had got to the part about grinding the beans—and it took Mrs. Drecker's startled shriek to alert them to the fact that they were not alone.

Adam had snatched up a dish towel and, blushing like a bride, held it in front of his hips as he sputtered an apology for being naked in his own kitchen. Mrs. Drecker, after one horrified, admiring look, had turned her back to them, her hands over her face for good measure. Daphne, giving a tiny gasp of surprise, had been convulsed with laughter.

"Oh, Adam! The look on your face!" she said, still giggling helplessly as they stumbled into the bedroom. "The look on *her* face! You'd think she'd never seen a naked man before. And you, backing down the hall with that dinky little towel in front of your... your privates. You looked so... so..." She collapsed onto the bed, holding her sides as the laughter shook her, making it impossible to speak.

Adam shot her a reproving look, but there was a smile tugging at the corners of his mouth. "It isn't *that* funny," he said, trying to sound stern.

"Oh, yes it is," Daphne sputtered, pushing herself up to a sitting position as she struggled to get control of herself. "You looked so shocked! As if—" she wiped at her streaming eyes "—as if your virtue had been violated." The thought sent her into fresh peals of laughter.

Adam's smile broke through. "Do you think she'll quit?" he asked, eyes twinkling.

"Oh, no! Not—" she hiccuped "—not as long as there's a chance of catching you in the buff again."

"Daphne!"

"You mark my words," Daphne teased. "She'll be coming in extra early from now on, hoping to catch you in—"

Adam threw a pillow at her.

The doorbell rang again, pulling Daphne back to the present. Still smiling, she finished buckling her belt and hurried across the living room to the front door.

"Mrs. Drecker," she said, starting to speak before the door was halfway open. It wasn't Mrs. Drecker. "Oh, Sunny, come on in. I was hoping it was the cleaning lady. She's late this morning." She held out her arms to the toddler who was clutching the neckline of Sunny's T-shirt. "Hello, Mollie, me darlin'. How's my favorite redhead?"

The child changed hands willingly. "Mack," she said.

"Right this way." Daphne nuzzled Mollie's sweet powder-scented neck. "Come on to the bedroom." Daphne spoke around the child in her arms, leading the way down the short hall. "I haven't quite finished dressing."

"Isn't that a little, um, elegant for a protest?" Sunny said from behind her.

"That's just what I was wondering." She tossed Mollie onto the bed. "Don't bother Queenie," she warned. "It's been years since I've been to one so I wasn't sure what the current mode of dress is."

Wordlessly, Sunny raised her arms and turned, offering herself for inspection.

Daphne crossed her arms, head tilted consideringly as she took in Sunny's olive-green corduroy pants, camouflage T-shirt and Nike running shoes. She had a tomato-red cashmere sweater tied around her waist and a diamond the size of a small ice cube on the third finger of her left hand. Her inch-long nails were painted to match the sweater.

"Is that what every well-dressed radical is wearing these days? Camouflage and cashmere?"

"What? This old thing?" Sunny picked up a sleeve of her sweater. "Strictly utilitarian."

Daphne snorted and turned toward the mirror to fasten a pair of thin gold chains around her neck. The tiny star on one nestled in the soft hollow of her throat. "I guess I'll stick with what I've got on," she said, slipping a small gold hoop into her pierced ear. "If you can wear cashmere, I can certainly get away with flannel slacks. Besides—" she fastened on the other earring "—I've got to look at some office space this afternoon."

Sunny pounced on that immediately. "Office space? What office space? Are you finally moving Night Lights to San Francisco?"

"No, I'm not moving Night Lights to San Francisco," she replied, but that's *exactly* what she was thinking of doing—if things worked out the way she hoped they would. And there was no reason to think they wouldn't.

She and Adam had been getting along very well these past six weeks; their relationship was calmer than it had been eleven years ago. More sedate. No, not sedate, she thought, not liking the image that conjured up. Adult, that was the word. Yes, more adult. Adam had mellowed nicely and she had become much less volatile. They had both grown up. They were careful of each other's feelings. Solicitous of each other's opinions. Why, they hadn't had one argument in all the time they'd been seeing each other again. Not even a minor disagreement.

Was that normal, she wondered.

"So why are you looking for an office?" Sunny prompted when Daphne just stood there, staring into space.

Daphne's eyes refocused on the redhead. "What?"

"If you're not moving Night Lights, then why are you looking for an office?"

"Because, uh..." It took Daphne a minute to remember what they had been talking about. "Because I've been spending more and more time in San Francisco—" she paused, catching the look on Sunny's face "—*over the last year or so.*" She emphasized the last few words but they caused no change in Sunny's expression. If anything, the redhead's know-it-all grin got wider.

"All right, you can just wipe that smug, silly look off your face, Elizabeth McCorkle," Daphne said sternly, hands on her hips. "I've been thinking about opening a branch office out here for the last six months at least."

"Uh-huh," Sunny snorted.

"Well, I have! I have as many customers here as I do in New York, if not more. In fact, my line sells better in California than it does anywhere else. That's why I've made so many trips—"

"Uh-huh," Sunny said again, smirking.

"And it's much closer to Hong Kong," she pointed out. "So it will save me time and money in the long run. On freight and airfare and...so forth."

"Uh-huh."

"Well, dammit, I can't just keep spreading my stuff all over Adam's house," Daphne said, goaded into admitting the truth. Or, at least, part of it. "Mrs. Drecker is threatening to quit."

"Uh-huh."

"Well, she is!"

"I don't doubt that for a minute. Cleaning up after you has got to be one of the worst jobs in the world," Sunny conceded. "But—No, Mollie," she interrupted herself to correct her daughter. "Don't pull Mack's tail." She glanced back at Daphne, still grinning. "But that's not the reason you're relocating your business."

"*Thinking* of relocating."

"Whatever." Sunny waved a manicured hand dismissively and sat down on the edge of the unmade bed to gently disengage her daughter's chubby fingers from the cat's twitching tail. "Mommy said 'No,'" she admonished the child firmly and then looked up at Daphne, her expression serious and concerned. "Is it really so hard to admit that you're still crazy in love with Adam and you'd give your eyeteeth to be married to him again?"

"Who says I want to get married again?" Daphne hedged, not bothering to deny the first part of Sunny's statement. They both knew it was true. "I'm perfectly happy with the way things are," she lied valiantly. "We have a . . . a modern, adult relationship and I—"

"Bull!" Sunny said.

Daphne's eyebrows nearly disappeared into the curls on her forehead. "I beg your pardon?"

"You heard me. I said bu—"

"I heard what you said." Daphne inclined her head toward the child. "Mollie did too."

"Mollie's heard me swear before, haven't you, sweetheart? Quit trying to change the subject. You're no more satisfied with this so-called adult relationship than I would be."

"That's not true. I'm very satisfied with it."

"Are you?" Sunny challenged.

Daphne managed to hold the redhead's gaze for about ten seconds. "No," she said at last. "No, I *hate* it."

"Then why are you putting up with it? Why don't you just tell Adam that you're tired of playing transcontinental footsie and you want to get married."

Daphne sank down on the bed beside her friend, a little half laugh catching in her throat. "If only it were that simple!"

"Why isn't it that simple? You love Adam. Adam loves you. Ergo, wedding bells."

"Ergo, nothing. Yes, I love Adam. I've always loved Adam. And he loves me..." Her brow furrowed up in a frown. "I think," she tacked on, plucking at the crease of her flannel slacks with two fingers. "What he actually said was that he felt something *special* for me," she explained, recalling the conversation they'd had that night in his kitchen. "But that's not the point."

"So what is?"

"The point is, when Adam and I got married it was because I talked him into it. Remember? I wouldn't listen to any of his arguments against it. We were too young, too different. We'd be poor. But I thought nothing mattered except that we loved each other, and I badgered and coaxed and pleaded until I was hoarse." She sighed and shook her head. "I'm ashamed to admit it but I even tried using sex to get my way."

Sunny's brown eyes brightened with prurient curiosity. "Is that what finally did the trick?"

"In a backhanded sort of way." Daphne laughed softly, remembering. "Adam always thought that he shouldn't have been sleeping with me in the first place. I was only seventeen when we met, remember? And still pure as the driven snow in spite of all that smart talk about liberated womanhood and free love. I think he felt vaguely guilty about leading me down the path to wickedness." Her eyes sparkled gleefully for a moment. "Completely forgetting, of course, that the first time I practically had to push him into bed." Her shoulders lifted in a little shrug. "Anyway, when I threatened to cut him off until he married me, he said he thought abstinence was a good idea." She giggled, a delicious, utterly feminine sound. "And then I spent the next three days convincing him it wasn't."

"Sounds like fun."

"Mack gone," Mollie said mournfully, standing up on the bed to lean against her mother's shoulder. Sunny reached up and absently patted the little hand that had snaked its way around her neck.

"How did that get you married?" she asked Daphne.

"When Adam realized that we couldn't keep our hands off each other he decided it was best that we get married, after all. So we decided to elope."

"And?"

"And nothing. You know the rest. We were divorced in less than two years." She shook her head slightly, as if to clear it. "Anyway, to answer your first question. The reason Adam and I are having this 'adult relationship' is because it's sort of a... a trial," she said, putting it into words for the first time.

"What?" Sunny's start of surprise sent Mollie tumbling back against the bed. "You mean like a trial marriage?"

"Yes, I guess you could call it that."

"And Adam agreed?" Sunny couldn't seem to believe it. "Old straight-laced conservative Adam?"

"We're doing it, aren't we?" Daphne responded, needled by Sunny's implication that Adam would be the one to object to such an arrangement. She was partly right; Adam hadn't actually agreed to it. Not in so many words, anyway. But Daphne told herself that was only because they hadn't gotten around to discussing or defining exactly what it was they were doing. They were living together, true, but to what end? Adam hadn't said and Daphne hadn't asked. It was beginning to tell on her.

"We both agree that there's something, uh, special between us," she said then, trying to explain it to herself as well as Sunny. "So we're taking this time to find out what it is and—"

"It's called love," Sunny interrupted dryly.

"And if it will last," Daphne went on, ignoring the interruption. "We're getting to know each other again, finding out if we can be friends as well as lovers. If we can live together without driving each other crazy. Which is exactly why I have to find some office space," she concluded, coming to her feet as she spoke. "Or this little arrangement won't last long enough for us to find out."

She put her hand out and hauled Sunny to her feet. "Come on. Pick up that child and let's go to this protest of yours before I get smart and change my mind."

THERE WERE ALREADY twenty or so people milling around in front of the research center when Sunny pulled her yellow Mercedes station wagon up to the curb. They were mostly housewife types: nicely dressed matrons and young mothers pushing strollers or holding a child by the hand, or both. There were a few earnest-looking teenagers sprinkled among the women, a few senior citizens, a few middle-aged men.

A far cry, Daphne thought, from the long-haired, jean-clad, headband-wearing young rebels she had marched with in her early protest days. Not a fanatic among them, she decided, except, of course, for the ever fanatic Sunny McCorkle in her designer combat fatigues.

"Now what?" Daphne said as Sunny turned the wheels and set the parking brake.

"Now, we pass out the signs." She gestured over her shoulder. "There's a card table back there, too, for the petition. Jason will set that up." She waved at a young man, motioning him toward the back of the station wagon. "Why don't you get Mollie out of her car seat while I get the signs?"

"Fine," Daphne agreed, twisting around in her seat to liberate the three-year-old from her safety restraints. "Looks like it's you and me, kid," she said, lifting the child into her arms as she got out of the car. She leaned against the shiney yellow hood, bouncing Mollie against her hip, and watched while Sunny organized her troops.

She was as good at it as ever. In less than five minutes the former Student for a Democratic Society had everyone, babies and children included, wearing black armbands—mourning for the deceased animals, Daphne finally decided—and marching in close-order drill in front of the medical research center. Most of the protesters carried one of Sunny's hand-lettered signs. Stop Slaughtering Our Pets and Vivisection Is Killing Puppies seemed to be the two favorites. A few carried placards with rather gruesome representations of puppies and kittens and baby monkeys who had apparently been the unfortunate victims of medical research.

It was an emotional, heart-wrenching scene—as Sunny had fully intended it should be—because no one, no matter what side of the question they stood on or how important they believed the results of the research to be, wanted to think of their own beloved pet ending up as an experiment.

Daphne certainly didn't. She had listened to Brian McCorkle argue the pros and cons of the issue with his hardheaded, soft-hearted wife; she had heard Adam's views on the subject and was aware of the vast amount of valuable information that animal experimentation supplied to the medical world; she even agreed that some of it couldn't have been gathered in any other way. But, still, to think of Mack or Queenie or Tiger suffering untold pain in a lab such as this? It was unthinkable.

And that was why, despite some reservations, she had agreed to come today.

"Here, let me tie this around your arm," Sunny said, wrapping a strip of black cloth around Daphne's bicep. "You, too, sweetheart." She tied another one around Mollie's plump little arm, letting the ends dangle down the sleeve of her pink sweatshirt. For the first time Daphne noticed that the front of Mollie's sweatshirt sported a grinning dog face and the legend, I Love my Dachshund. Mollie didn't have a dachshund.

"Have you no shame?" Daphne chided mildly. "Using your own child as propaganda?"

"Mollie'd love her dachshund if she had one, wouldn't you, sweetheart?" Sunny said, taking the child from Daphne's arms. She passed her along to the young man standing beside her. "Hold on tight to Jason," she urged as he lifted Mollie to his shoulders.

Mollie clutched the young man's hair with both hands. "Gid'up," she ordered gleefully.

Jason whinnied and galloped to his place in the picket line.

Sunny thrust a sign into Daphne's hands and hoisted her own. "Come on, the TV crew should be here any minute."

"The TV crew?" Somewhat reluctantly Daphne followed Sunny into the line of protestors and began to shuffle along with them. "You didn't mention any TV crew when you were talking me into this thing."

"Didn't want to get your hopes up. Jason only found out this morning that they'd be here for sure. His girlfriend works in the station's film library," Sunny informed her, flashing a grin over her shoulder. "Isn't that great?"

"Great," Daphne echoed faintly.

The police arrived before the TV crew but they were, it seemed, only there as a precaution. Aside from warning the protesters not to block the sidewalk to passersby and not to physically harass anyone going in and out of the building, the police merely watched. And waited.

Daphne waited, too, shielding her face behind her picket sign, and hoped Jason's girlfriend had been wrong. She wasn't. The TV crew arrived ten minutes later, their sky-blue van marked with the station's call letters.

At a signal from Sunny, the protesters began to chant louder, thrusting their signs into the air with increasing enthusiasm as the Minicam zoomed in on them.

"Excuse me, ma'am," a reporter said, thrusting a microphone under Daphne's nose. "Could you tell us what you hope to gain by this demonstration?"

Daphne shook her head and ducked behind her sign, pointing a mocha-tipped finger at the back of Sunny's head. "Ask her," she mumbled.

"Excuse me, ma'am..." The well-mannered reporter repeated her question, directing it to Sunny.

"We hope to arouse public concern for what's going on in that—" she gestured over her shoulder and shuddered dramatically "—that torture chamber there."

"Torture chamber? Could you elaborate on that, please?"

Sunny was glad to elaborate. It was one of her favorite things. "Helpless animals are being systematically tortured and mutilated in the name of medical research."

"Don't you think that's a bit strong?" the reporter questioned. "You make it sound like a concentration camp for animals when, in fact—"

"Isn't that what it is? A concentration camp?" Sunny interrupted, jumping on the reporter's choice of words with relish. "Tell me what else you would call it when perfectly healthy cats and dogs—*children's pets*—are being purchased from city pounds to be used in painful, crippling and unnecessary experiments."

"Poor puppy," Mollie said mournfully, her high childish voice clearly audible over the noise of the crowd. The reporter—and the Minicam—turned their attention to the adorable redheaded three-year-old sitting on Jason's shoulders.

"Do you have a pet, honey?" the reporter said gently, holding the microphone up to Mollie's lips. "What's your dachshund's name?" she added, taking her cue from the front of Mollie's pink sweatshirt.

"Poor puppy," Mollie repeated, her bottom lip out. "Poor, poor puppy." She was shaking her head sadly.

"Shame on you!" Daphne hissed in Sunny's ear as the reporter turned to face the camera, wrapping up her story. "Teaching that child to tell lies."

"What lies?" Sunny hissed back, brown eyes wide and innocent. "All she said was 'poor puppy.' She didn't say she had one."

"... this is Karen Zachary, reporting live from the Hillman Medical Research Center." The Minicam was lowered, the reporter and her crew hurried back across the street to the blue van that was double-parked.

Sunny handed her placard to one of the other protesters and opened her arms, lifting Molly from Jason's shoulders. "Mommy's brilliant little girl," she said delightedly, nuzzling the child's neck.

"Poor puppy," Mollie said again, playing it for all it was worth. "Poo-oor puppy."

"Yes, poor puppy. But that's enough now, sweetheart. The cameras are all gone. Say goodbye to Jason."

"Bye, Jason," Mollie repeated obediently, throwing him a sloppy kiss over her mother's shoulder.

"Does this mean we're leaving now?" Daphne asked, following the energetic pair of redheads to the car. "That's it? Five minutes in front of the cameras is all the protesting you're going to do? Elizabeth McCorkle, I'm surprised at you!"

"Why?" Sunny spoke over her shoulder as she strapped Mollie into her car seat. "I've done my part here today. Jason and some of the others will stay for most of the afternoon and try to get some more signatures on that petition."

"And just what was your part?" asked Daphne curiously, pulling open her own door as Sunny went around to the driver's side.

"Focusing media attention on an issue of vital importance," Sunny said promptly, speaking to her over the roof of the car. "By giving that reporter something more interesting to film than a bunch of people carrying signs, I've practically assured our cause a spot on the nightly news. That means public attention will be focused on this research center."

"And?"

"And maybe we can stop what's going on in there." She waved at Jason, giving him a smile and a thumbs-up sign and slid behind the wheel. Daphne scrambled into her own seat. "Now," Sunny said, gunning the engine to life. "Where shall I drop you?"

11

ADAM'S FOREST-GREEN BMW was already in the driveway when Daphne's taxi pulled up in front of his Russian Hill address.

Damn, she thought, as she opened her purse to pay the driver. *One of the few days Adam gets home from the hospital before six o'clock and I'm not here to greet him.* The perfect opportunity to show him what suitable doctor's wife material she had turned into down the drain because of a rental agent's faulty transmission.

Well, if she was lucky, she thought, he had only just come in himself. Maybe the evening could still be salvaged and she could begin her new campaign. Quick-like-a-bunny, she could change into one of her slinky at-home outfits, bring him a glass of wine while he watched the evening news, ask him about his day, make him a nice dinner, supposing, of course, that there was anything in the refrigerator to make a nice dinner with.

And so Operation Wife begins with a whimper, she thought, frowning to herself as she pushed open the iron gate at the end of the front walk.

She hurried up the uneven brick path, mentally reviewing the contents of said refrigerator, and inserted her key into the lock on the front door. Holding her breath, she pushed it open and peeked in. The living room was clean and tidy. Mrs. Drecker hadn't quit yet.

"Thank God for small favors," Daphne mumbled as she let herself in and closed the door behind her. "At least Adam didn't come home to a *dirty* empty house."

She started to toss her purse on the sofa and then, thinking better of it, tucked it under her arm and continued down the hall toward the low hum of voices coming from the bedroom.

Fresh from the shower, Adam was stretched out on top of the striped bedspread, propped up on the pile of pillows stacked against the teak headboard. His long hairy legs, bare from the mid-thigh down, were crossed at the ankle. A wedge of his equally hairy chest was exposed between the open edges of a white terry bathrobe. He was surrounded by cats. Mack, the feline ragmop, lay sprawled across Adam's stomach like a fat orange throw rug. Queenie, the aloof one, was perched on the headboard behind him. Tiger sat on the bedside table with his paw in a ceramic bowl, furtively fishing for an M&M.

"Hi," Adam said, looking up as she entered the room. "You're just in time. Sunny called a few minutes ago and said to be sure to tell you to watch the evening news." He popped an M&M in his mouth with a careless flick of his wrist. "I was just getting set to get up and tape it for you but this is much better." His smile was warm and welcoming. "Come watch with me," he invited, holding out his hand. "There's plenty of M&Ms for everybody."

Daphne dropped her purse on the floor and stepped out of her shoes. "Best offer I've had all day," she quipped, crawling across the bed to cuddle up in the warm curve of Adam's outstretched arm. It closed around her, drawing her in. "Umm." She snuggled against his side. "Heaven."

"Don't I get a kiss hello?"

Daphne tilted her face to look up at him. "Depends. Do I get one of those M&Ms you promised me?"

He reached sideways into the ceramic bowl, gently batting Tiger's paw out of the way, and held one up in front of her. "Trade?"

Daphne tilted her head further back, eyes closed, and opened her mouth.

The kiss was deep and satisfying and quickly threatened to develop into something more. Adam's big body shifted toward hers, turning as if to envelope her in an even closer embrace.

Mack dug his claws in, protesting the move.

Adam fell back. "Damn cat's trying to emasculate me," he said without heat, and dropped the M&M into Daphne's open mouth.

Daphne chewed and swallowed before answering. "Get tough," she suggested, threading her fingers through the golden whorls of hair on Adam's chest. "Tell him to move."

"Move," Adam ordered, wiggling his hips a little in an effort to dislodge the cat. Mack opened one yellow eye to see what all the commotion was about. Adam wiggled his hips again. Disgruntled, the cat rose, stretched languidly and thoroughly, and stalked off to the more settled regions at the foot of the bed.

"You're so forceful." Daphne sighed heavily, as if in breathless admiration. "And I'm such a sucker for forceful men." Her hand feathered lower, plucking delicately at the fine hairs around Adam's navel.

Adam's stomach muscles contracted. "So you like forceful men, do you?" He growled playfully and turned toward her, one hand reaching between them to push her hand even further down his stomach. "I'll show you forceful."

Daphne giggled, her eyes going golden with anticipation and sudden desire. "Promise?"

His mouth came down on hers just as her fingers closed around him. Daphne felt him jerk, his muscles tightening in reaction to her touch, and then his tongue invaded her mouth, filling her with the taste of him. It was a long sweet moment before either of them moved except to press closer.

"I missed you today," he murmured, his mouth a mere fraction of an inch from hers. "All day I thought about you. About this." He moved his hips against her hand. "It played hell with my concentration."

A part of Daphne thrilled to his words, but another part of her stood back, hoping for more. He missed her, he wanted her, but did he love her? She *thought* he did, hoped he did, but in the past six weeks he had never said the words. Not even in the so-called "throes of passion" had he gone so far as to declare his love for her. And Daphne needed to hear it. Needed it with every fiber of her being. Because, until he said the words, she wouldn't be free to say them, either. She had pushed him down the road to commitment and matrimony once. She wouldn't do it again.

"I missed you, too," she said softly, striving for lightness with a voice that was husky with suppressed emotion. Then she pulled his head back down to hers, afraid that if her lips were free, she might say the words he wasn't ready to hear.

"Helpless animals are being systematically tortured and mutilated in the name of medical research." Sunny's voice, clear and confident, broke through their building passion.

"The TV," Daphne murmured, shifting a little beneath him.

"Hmm?" Adam lifted his head a bit, turning to squint over his shoulder at the television.

"Perfectly healthy dogs and cats—*children's pets*—are being purchased from city pounds to be used in painful, crippling and unnecessary experiments."

"Oh, God, Sunny's on the warpath again!" Adam chuckled and levered himself from Daphne's supine form. He lifted her a little more upright, holding her in the crook of his arm so she could see the television, too. "I wonder if poor Brian knew what screwball thing she was up to today."

Daphne cringed at his words, and hoped that the camera hadn't caught her face, too. It was one thing to want a little more discussion between them, and quite another that something like this should be the focus of that discussion. She wanted to *talk* to Adam, not fight with him. And her protesting activities had always started them fighting.

"Poor puppy," Mollie piped up right on cue and the camera zoomed in for a close-up, focusing on the cherubic little face of the youngest McCorkle.

Adam hooted. "Will you look at that! She's got Mollie in the act, too. Brian's going to be fit to be tied."

"Do you really think he'll be angry?" Daphne began hesitantly. "I mean it *is* a good cause . . . isn't it?" she said hopefully, already knowing his views.

Adam shook his head, his eyes on the TV screen. "Animal research is absolutely vital to the advancement of medical science. And if Sunny would stop letting her emotions rule her head for a minute, she'd realize it."

"Poor, poor puppy." Mollie's lower lip quivered right into the camera. The picture widened to include the message on her pink sweatshirt.

Adam laughed again. "You've got to admire that crazy redhead, though. Using Mollie was a masterstroke," he said, motioning toward the screen with his free hand. "That reporter played right into her hands."

The camera angle changed again, slowly panning back to bring the reporter—and the protesters—into full view.

Daphne's body stiffened slightly, anticipating the explosion.

"Good God, that's you!" Adam shot upright on the bed, his eyes fastened to the screen. Daphne bounced against the mattress as his arm came out from under her.

For just a moment, Daphne considered denying it. She took another quick look at the screen. No way around it, she thought, the woman standing directly behind Sunny McCorkle, with her hands wrapped around a particularly grisly placard was none other than herself. She was speaking into the redhead's ear, looking for all the world as if she were whispering instructions.

"Yes, I guess it is," she admitted reluctantly, struggling to sit up among the pillows.

"This is Karen Zachary, reporting live from the Hillman Medical Research Center."

The screen faded into a close-up of the anchorman back at the studio. "Thank you for that report, Karen," he said, smiling into the camera. The newscast faded into a commercial.

Adam turned to look at Daphne. "I didn't know you were going to be involved in that today," he said calmly.

"I didn't either," Daphne hurried to explain. "That is, I knew I was going because Sunny asked me to, I just didn't know about the reporter and—"

"Hey." Adam halted her with a quick shake of his head. "You don't owe me any explanations. You're a free agent, remember? You can get involved in as many, er, causes," he said judiciously, "as you want to. It has nothing to do with me." He swung his feet to the floor. "So, what do you say we go get something to eat?" he said, retying the sash on his robe as he looked down at her.

The subject, she realized, was most definitely closed. Instead of yelling at her as he would have eleven years ago, instead of telling her what an idiot she was making of herself by getting involved in another crazy bleeding heart cause, instead of demanding that she get herself *uninvolved*, he very calmly said that it had nothing to do with him. Why was he being so damn reasonable and polite?

Didn't he care what she did?

Daphne sat upright, curling her legs under her, Indian fashion. "I thought we might eat in tonight," she said, her voice as calm as his. *Like a married couple*, she added silently.

"Sure, if you like. What did you have in mind?"

"Oh, I don't know." Daphne picked at the striped bedspread with two fingernails. "Whatever's in the kitchen."

Adam looked doubtful. "I don't think there's much of a choice." He headed for the bedroom door with a purposeful stride. "But I'll see what I have."

Daphne came up off the bed in a rush. "Oh, no. I didn't mean for you to make it, Adam. You've been working hard all day and... well." She shrugged. "I just feel like doing something domestic tonight, that's all."

"Domestic? You?"

Daphne scowled at him. "I get these impulses once in a while, you know. Even I can get tired of eating out all the time."

"We could order something in," he suggested.

"I get tired of that, too," Daphne said, wondering why he still seemed so intent on treating her like a guest when she had, for all intents and purposes, been living with him for the past six weeks.

Her "few" clothes took up half his closet space, she had completely taken over two of his six dresser drawers and was nudging him out of a third, the tools of her trade were littered over his dining room table, her cats left their hair all over his furniture, and her friends, both the "crazy radicals" and the "flaky fashion types," left their messages on his answering machine.

And Adam still seemed to think that she had to be taken out to dinner every night as if she were a weekend guest. *That* was a misconception that she wanted changed. Now. He would never begin to think of her as a wife, of remarriage, if he continued to think of her as a guest in his home.

"Why don't you just relax. Here on the bed," she invited, leaning over to plump the pillows back up. "Let *me* see what's in the kitchen. Come on." She took his arm and propelled him back to the bed. "Relax. Let Dan Rather tell you what's going on in the world." She reached out and plucked the ceramic bowl off the bedside table. "Have some more M&Ms," she advised, putting it into his hands. "I'll get you a nice glass of white wine."

"With M&Ms?"

"So, I'll get you a glass of rosé," she said airily. "It goes with everything."

She exited the room with as much grace as possible and then raced down the hall to the kitchen. The refrigerator was better stocked than the first time she had looked into it, but not by much. A quart of cream, several half-full foil-covered cans of Seafood Supper, Creamed Kidney Bits and Chicken Nibbles, a carton of eggs, a closed plastic container with a selection of cheeses, three different kinds of deli meat wrapped in waxed paper, a loaf of sourdough bread, unopened jars of pickles and olives, a six-pack of imported beer, several bottles of wine; all the ingredients for tomorrow's picnic but not, she thought despondently, the makings of a great meal.

"Noodles," she said to herself, remembering having seen a package tucked into one of the cupboards. She could make a halfway decent fettuccine Alfredo with those noodles and what was on hand in the refrigerator. The cats would just do without their cream tomorrow morning.

She filled a large pan full of water and set it on the stove. Opening a bottle of the promised rosé, she set it on a tray with two long-stemmed glasses and carried it back into the bedroom.

"Dan Rather's on vacation," Adam said with a sheepish grin, explaining in advance why the TV was now tuned in to reruns of *The Love Boat*.

Daphne flashed him a knowing look and set the tray on the bedside table. "You have the most juvenile taste in TV shows," she said, pouring out a glass of wine. "Well, enjoy." She handed it to him with a flourish. "I'm going to go take a quick shower while the water's boiling."

Adam looked up at her with a hopeful leer. "Need some help?"

"I said a *quick* shower."

But her shower wasn't as quick as she'd planned. She couldn't find the shower cap so her hair got wet and she ended up washing it. Which meant drying it, too. And then she decided that her legs needed shaving. Finally, lotioned and powdered and perfumed, she slipped a silky peach-colored caftan over her head. It had a wide V-neck, fluttery split sleeves that fastened with a small satin frog on each shoulder and a hem that brushed against her ankles when she walked. It was also very nearly transparent.

Deftly, she touched up her makeup and fluffed up her hair. *The very picture of wifely devotion*, she decided, grinning at herself in the mirror.

Despite a slight delay, she had finally managed to put her plan into action. Adam had his glass of wine, she had slipped into something slinky, dinner was well on its way to being done. All she had to do now was get him to talk about his work. And, since Adam loved his work, that should be no problem at all, she thought, stepping out of the steamy bathroom.

No problem at all except that Adam was sound asleep. The wineglass, empty now, tilted precariously from his right hand. Mack had crawled back up on his stomach and lay sprawled in feline abandon. Tiger was sleeping in the crook of his bent elbow, his pointed little face looking ridiculously sweet against the hard curve of Adam's bicep. Queenie, as usual, was close by but held herself apart form the rest of the hoi polloi.

Daphne stood silently for a few moments, disappointment building inside her. Then she sighed in resignation and moved across the carpet on bare feet. They would have all day tomorrow together, she reminded herself.

Gently, she eased the wineglass from between Adam's slack fingers and placed it on the tray. He mumbled something unintelligible and shifted his weight on the bed. Daphne waited a minute, holding her breath until he—and the cats—settled in again, and then she clicked off the remote control, sending the television into darkness. Adam didn't stir. She snapped off the lamp and left the room.

In the kitchen, the pot of water was boiling furiously on the stove, half of its volume already vaporized into steam. Daphne turned it off and put the parmesan cheese and cream she had got out back in the refrigerator. If Adam woke up later and was hungry it would be easy enough to get things started again. But she didn't think he'd wake up. The tiredness had been deeply etched into his sleeping face.

He pushed himself too hard, she thought, thinking of the long hours he spent at the hospital and the many, many times the phone or his beeper had called him back there when she had thought he was through for the day.

How many times in the last six weeks had he been called away from dinner or a movie or a cuddle in front of the fire by that damn electronic leash of his? And how many times had she stifled her impatience because of it? Enough times, she thought with a little start of surprise, so that she rarely felt the impatience now. She was getting used to it, she realized, accepting it as part of the total package that was Dr. Adam Forrest.

She was learning to know Adam, she thought; learning to accept him just as he was, warts and all; learning that his intense dedication to his work, his drive and ambition, were as much a part of him as his hard golden body. She was, she decided happily, learning to relate to Adam as a friend and companion as well as the lover who made her blood run hot with just a glance.

She wondered if he was learning to accept her, too. He seemed to but he hadn't said, and afraid of his answer, she hadn't asked. But there was time enough for that, she concluded. More than time enough. She'd start acting wifelike in the morning, and pretty soon Adam would start feeling more like a husband. It would only be a short step from feeling like a husband to wanting to be one again, wouldn't it?

With a yawn, Daphne flicked off the bedroom light and went back down the hall to the bedroom. She pushed her caftan off her shoulders, letting it slide down her body to the floor. And naked, except for the two thin gold chains around her neck, she slipped under the covers next to Adam.

A good wife, she thought, grinning wickedly, would be there when he woke up.

12

"WAKE UP, SLEEPING BEAUTY." Daphne leaned over the figure on the bed, waving a cup of freshly brewed coffee back and forth in the general vicinity of Adam's nose.

His nostrils twitched, as if catching the scent, but he didn't wake. He lay sprawled on his back in his favorite position, arm and legs flung out in every direction, a vagrant lock of hair falling over his forehead. The brown sheet was pulled up to his breastbone, making the exposed skin of his shoulders and arms look even more golden than usual in contrast.

My sleeping Greek god, she thought tenderly, feeling the urge to reach out and brush the hair back from his forehead.

Instead, she blew gently across the top of the cup, sending the fragrant steam into Adam's face. "I've got coffee," she singsonged. "Wake up."

Adam's nostrils twitched again, narrowing as he inhaled deeply. "Coffee?" he said groggily, and rolled to his side. The sheet caught under him as he moved, slipping down to his waist. He opened one blue eye, focusing on the cup in her hand. "You make it?" he mumbled.

"Uh-huh," Daphne assured him, nodding. "Fresh this morning."

His eye closed. "Don't want it then," he muttered into his pillow.

"Okay." Her shoulders lifted in a careless shrug. "I guess I'll just take it back to the kitchen and pour it out," she threatened cheerfully, turning as if to leave.

Adam's hand shot out, grabbing a fistful of her silky caftan. "Wait," he ordered, eyes still closed against the morning. "Changed my mind." He pulled on the caftan, tugging until she was forced to sit down on the edge of the bed.

"Careful, Adam," she warned, covering the top of the cup with her free hand as she sank to the mattress. "You'll make me spill it."

"Put it down," he suggested, rolling over onto his back again. His eyes were fully open now, but still deceptively sleepy looking as they wandered over her body in the low-necked, tissue-thin, silk caftan. Daphne recognized the expression immediately.

"Oh, no, you don't," she said, laughing as she shook her head at him. "You promised we'd go to the park today. Have a picnic, remember?"

Silently, still smiling that sexy sleepy little smile of his, Adam took the coffee cup from her with his right hand, reaching sideways to place it on the bedside table.

"You mentioned roller-skating, too," she reminded him. "And then maybe some shopping in Ghirardelli Square."

His left arm curled around her back, drawing her down. Daphne put her hands on his shoulders, elbows stiff as she pretended to resist. The loose open neckline of her caftan slid halfway down her arm, completely baring her left shoulder and breast. Daphne ignored it.

"Then there was dinner at that new Chinese place you were telling me about and dancing at—"

"Hmm," Adam said, his arm tightening across her back until her elbows bent and her forearms were pressing against his chest. "We will." His lips touched her bare shoulder. "Later."

"Uh-huh," Daphne scoffed, still trying to hold him off. "How much later?"

Adam grinned lazily. "About thirty minutes later?" he suggested and lifted his head from the pillow to touch his lips to the upper slope of her bared breast.

Daphne sighed, melting against him like hot wax against a candle flame. "Only thirty minutes?"

Adam laughed softly, deep in his chest, and rolled over, carrying Daphne with him so that she ended up on her back beneath him, her legs trapped by the sheet that had been covering his golden body, her arms held to her sides by the weight of his chest and the way her caftan was pulled down off one shoulder. His left arm was still wrapped around her back, causing her spine to arch, thrusting her breasts forward like an offering.

"We'll take as long as you want," he promised, his voice no longer teasing as his eyes made a slow, thorough survey of her lush breasts. The right one was only lightly veiled, the pale brown nipple and surrounding areola clearly visible beneath the thin silk of the peach caftan. The left breast was totally bared to his heated gaze.

He moved his right hand, cupping her exposed breast in his palm, and lowered his head. He took the puckered nipple into the warmth of his mouth, laving it with quick little flicks of his tongue. It hardened instantly, drawing up, tightening, aching for a firmer pressure. Instinctively, seeming to know just what she needed, Adam began to suckle more strongly, his cheeks flexing as he took as much of her breast into his mouth as he could.

Daphne arched even further off the mattress, lifting up to him, feeling the sensual, primal pull of his mouth all the way to her womb. She moaned softly, her trapped hands seeking a way to touch him.

Adam lifted his head. "What?" he murmured, his hot breath rippling against her skin.

"I can't move," she breathed. "Can't touch you."

Adam shifted his weight immediately, turning and lifting her body until she lay on top of him. "Better?"

"Hmm, yes. Much." She sat up in one fluid motion, her knees sliding open to straddle his hips. With a sensuous little roll of her shoulder, she dropped the right side of her caftan and slipped both arms out of the loose fluttery sleeves.

She looked both elegant and sensual sitting there astride him, her long smooth torso rising up out of the peach silk draped around her hips. Her skin was soft and smooth, gleaming with good health and excellent care. The morning light coming in through the window seemed to play over the hills and valleys of her body, emphasizing her narrow waist, highlighting the lush fullness of her creamy breasts and the rounded curve of her shoulders, causing the tiny gold star in the hollow of her throat to glimmer with each breath she took.

Adam lay passive for a moment, drinking her in with his eyes, and then he raised his hands to her waist. His long surgeon's fingers fanned out across the lower curve of her back, urging her down.

Daphne resisted with a subtle, almost imperceptible shake of her head. Smiling softly, she reached out to touch him. Fingertips only at first, her nails scraped lightly over his tiny male nipples, making his skin ripple with a convulsive little shiver. Then her hands flattened, fingers spread wide, and she caressed the warm solid width of his hair-covered chest. Slowly, her eyes wide and golden as they followed the movement of her hands, she smoothed her palms over the hard curve of his shoulders and down the gentle bulge of his biceps.

Adam's hands began to move against her skin, sliding down under the peach silk to curve around the swell of her hips. His thumbs touched the soft, curling hair that hid the secrets of her body.

Daphne's eyes lifted, meeting his, and her palms continued their slow sensuous trek, smoothing over the hair-roughened sinews of his forearms until they came to rest on the backs of his hands, stopping them. For a moment she hovered there, her hands covering his, suspended in the web of his heated, hungering gaze, devouring him with a heated gaze of her own.

Then Adam's hands tightened under hers, demanding, and Daphne surged forward, called to him by something primitive and timeless. She pressed her soft full breasts to Adam's chest, her belly to his belly, her lips to his lips.

As if in slow motion, Adam rolled over again, pressing her down into the mattress. His mouth took hers in a gently savage kiss and his hands feathered up her sides and palmed her breasts, kneading their fullness with gentle skill. Urgently, maddeningly, his hips ground into the cradle of her open thighs, tempting her with that part of him that was still separated from her by the thin layers of peach silk and crisp brown sheets.

Daphne whimpered slightly, wanting more, wanting it all, and her hands reached down to push at the tangle of percale and silk that kept him from her. Adam lifted himself off her, turning to one side to help her rid them of this last impediment to their lovemaking. Then he was on her again, entering her slowly, moving slowly, driving her slowly mad.

Daphne ran her hands down his sleek back, her nails scraping lightly along the indentation of his spine, reveling in the feel of the muscles that rolled beneath her fingers with each slow thrust of his hips. She smoothed her palms down the slight inward slope at the small of his back and over the hard curve of his buttocks. There her fingers tightened, pressing, urging him to a more frantic pace. But Adam refused to be hurried. Refused to be pushed into the mindless passion of that first frantic reunion.

Perversely, Daphne wanted him to hurry, wanted to push him, wanted him to be so driven by desire that he lost his marvelous, maddening control. She wanted him so filled with hunger for her that he forget to be gentle and tender and caring of her pleasure. She wanted him, in short, to be as lost in their loving as she was.

And he wasn't.

Even as he moved within her, even as he whispered soft, sexy words into the damp curve of her neck, she could feel him holding back some essential part of himself. Feel him hiding... something... behind the expertise of his loving. But she was too far gone to figure out what that something was. Her hips bucked beneath him, urging, hungry, out of control.

"That's it," he murmured into her mouth. "Let it go. Let it come," he urged, retaining his control, his awareness of self and place, to the end, holding back until she had cried out in mindless pleasure... once, twice. And then, deliberately, he let go, thrusting forward into her welcoming body with a fierce cry of his own.

It was wonderful. It was satisfying. It left her sated and replete. But it wasn't the same as if he, too, had gone beyond control, had forgotten himself, lost himself, in loving her.

They lay tangled together for a moment more, panting lightly into each others' necks, letting the world right itself around them, and then Adam levered himself up and off her and rolled over onto his back.

"I bet my coffee's gotten cold," he said, grinning at her out of the corner of his eye.

For just a moment, the space of a heartbeat only, Daphne contemplated grabbing the cup and pouring its contents over his head. That he could lie there looking so normal and natural and so... so *relaxed, dammit,* while she was still trembling inside from the strength of her response, made her want to scream. *How can you be so blasé about something so earth-shattering,* she wanted to shout at him. *Don't you care?*

Instead, she calmly leaned over his supine body and stuck the tip of her index finger in the coffee cup. "Still warm," she said, drawing back with the cup in her hand. "Here." She set it down on his chest, waiting until he had put a steadying hand on it, and slithered off the bed. "Drink it. I'm going to take a shower."

"Coffee should be hot," he informed her, pulling himself up against the pillows. He took a quick sip and made a face. "Especially *your* coffee."

Daphne gave him a look over her shoulder. "It *was* hot," she said, and disappeared into the bathroom.

She came out twenty minutes later to find Adam still sprawled across the bed in all his naked glory, watching cartoons. The cats, with the exception of Mack who was probably still in the kitchen eating whatever the other two hadn't, were sprawled out beside him.

"Haven't we played this scene before?" she said whimsically, crossing his field of vision in all *her* naked glory on the way to the dresser.

"What scene?" Adam tried to watch Daphne as she bent over to open a drawer and keep his eye on the antics of Bugs Bunny and friends at the same time.

"Me coming out of the shower," Daphne said, stepping into a silky little teddy with a brown and tan leopard-skin pattern. She adjusted the straps on her shoulders, bending over to make sure the cups held her breasts just so. The fine chains around her neck caught the light as she moved, the tiny star glittering at the base of her throat. "You watching cartoons."

"I'm not watching cartoons," Adam denied, and he wasn't—now. "I'm watching you."

"Well, stop watching me," Daphne chided, pretending disapproval. "It only gives you ideas."

Adam wiggled his eyebrows suggestively. "Aren'cha glad?"

Daphne laughed, shaking her head at him, and disappeared into the closet. She came out a few minutes later shrugging into the top half of a khaki-colored safari jumpsuit made of lightweight cotton poplin. It had shoulder epaulets, cuffed elbow-length sleeves and a belt that neatly defined her narrow waist.

"You can watch one more cartoon," she said, watching him in the mirror as she adjusted the collar of the jumpsuit so that it stood up against the back of her neck. "Then you have to get up and get yourself into that shower."

"Are you going to come scrub my back?"

"No." She smiled at him in the mirror, head tilted as she inserted a large plain gold hoop in her earlobe. "I'm going to finish packing our picnic lunch." She inserted the other earring and then reached up, fluffing her hair. "And if you're not ready when I'm finished—" she turned toward the bed, an expression of mock sternness on her face "—I'm leaving without you. Is that clear?"

Adam threw a stiff salute, his body snapping to attention on the bed. "Yes, ma'am, perfectly clear."

Daphne struggled not to laugh. "One cartoon," she warned, shaking her finger at him as she left the bedroom.

Designing Woman 181

The telephone rang while whe was trying to fit a second bottle of wine into the picnic basket.

She let it ring, some sixth sense telling her that it was the hospital. Adam, she knew, would answer it from the bedroom extension. He picked it up halfway through the third ring. Five minutes later he came bustling out to the kitchen, a worried look shadowing his handsome face.

Daphne had already put the wine back in the refrigerator and was unloading the picnic basket.

"That was the hospital," he said unnecessarily, shrugging into a tan suede sport coat as he spoke. "Tiffany Jenkins has developed an infection." The little girl had had her third skin graft operation less than a week ago. "I've got to go. I—" He caught sight of the picnic basket, the cellophane-wrapped sandwiches, the little plastic containers of olives and carrot sticks on the counter. A guilty flush stole over his face. "The picnic! Damn!" He ran a hand through his hair. "I'm sorry, Daffy, but this is important and I've got—"

"You've got to go to the hospital. I know." She lifted a plastic container of pickles out of the basket and laid it on the counter beside the rest of the food.

Adam stood there speechless, not knowing what to say.

"Hey, it's all right," she said, forcing a bright little smile past the lump of disappointment in her throat. "I understand."

Adam looked skeptical.

"Really, I do." She left off what she was doing and came to him, putting her hands on the front of the muted blue-and-tan plaid sportshirt beneath his coat. "Tiffany Jenkins has an infection. You're her doctor." Her palms rubbed lightly over the shirt in a quick nervous little gesture. "You have to go."

Adam put his hands on her shoulders, knees slightly bent as he tried to look into her face. "You sure you don't mind?"

"Of course I *mind*," Daphne said, staring into his shirt front. "But I understand." Her eyes lifted for a moment, touching him, then dropped, lids fluttered as she struggled against the foolish childish tears of disappointment that threatened to overflow. "Really," she added, trying to convince them both that it was true.

"And you're not mad?" Adam's voice was still doubtful.

"No, I'm not mad," she denied. *For God's sake, Daphne, try to act like a reasonable adult! A canceled picnic isn't the end of the world. Reassure him.* She looked up, forcing a smile worthy of Donna Reed at her most wifely. "I'm disappointed, that's all." Her shoulders lifted in a little shrug as she twisted a button on his shirt front. "I was looking forward to spending the whole day with you. Just the two of us, alone, without any hospitals or fashion people or... anything."

"I know." Adam squeezed her shoulders. "I was looking forward to it, too," he said, but his words were perfunctory, his mind already halfway to the hospital and the problem he would find there.

Daphne hooked her hands over the outside of his arms, sliding them up to rest on his where he touched her shoulders. "Maybe you won't be all day?" she asked hopefully.

"It's hard to say. Maybe. It depends on exactly what the problem is." His attention was focused inward, thinking about all the different things that could have caused his patient's setback. She could tell he was anxious to be off.

Her hands dropped from his. "You'd better get going," she said in a flat little voice, that wifely, reassuring little smile still plastered to her face.

Adam seemed to shake himself back to the here-and-now. "Yes, I guess I'd better." He squeezed her shoulders again, more warmly than before. "Don't dismantle the picnic completely. If I don't get back in time today, we can always use it tomorrow." He leaned down and pressed a quick distracted kiss on her lips. "And we'll go out for dinner tonight no matter what, okay?"

"Okay," Daphne echoed hollowly, following him to the front door. She opened it for him, both hands holding it as he went out.

He turned back suddenly, hesitating. "I really am sorry about this, Daffy. I—" he struggled with the words "—I wanted this day together as much as you did."

Daphne nodded, her head against the edge of the door. "I know," she said, trying to believe it.

He looked for a moment as if he wanted to say something more, something... important. Instead, he reached out, curling his hand around the back of her head, and lifted her into his kiss. It wasn't quick. It wasn't distracted. It was long and thorough and turned Daphne's knees to jelly. "I'll be home as soon as I can," he whispered against her lips. "Wait for me."

Her childish resentment melted away at his words. Oh, the disappointment was still there, but somehow, knowing Adam was disappointed, too, made it easier to bear.

She wandered back into the kitchen when her legs could finally support her again and finished dealing with the contents of the picnic basket. Remembering Adam's instructions, she merely transferred everything, still neatly wrapped, to a shelf in the refrigerator. She was skeptical that Adam would be back in time to make a picnic feasible that afternoon—once he got to the hospital he wouldn't be back for hours—but maybe tomorrow.

She went back into the bedroom then, intending to do a little light housekeeping. Mrs. Drecker wouldn't be in again until Monday, and a whole weekend of not picking up after herself would make Adam's lovely house look like the proverbial tornado had hit it.

"You guys can have it back in a minute," she told the cats, shooing them off so she could make the bed. The results weren't quite in league with Mrs. Drecker's, she decided when she'd finished, but at least it was made. And the cats didn't seem to care about the less-than-professional results. They clambered back up on the bed, settling in for their midmorning nap before she'd tucked the bedspread up over the pillows.

She picked her silk caftan up off the floor, smiling a little as she thought about the activities that had led to its less than pristine condition, and headed for the bathroom to clean up in there. The phone rang for the second time that morning, surprising her with yesterday's clothes bundled up in her arms. She came out of the bathroom, dropped the rumpled clothes on a convenient chair, and headed for the ringing phone.

"Hello?" She sat down on the bed as she spoke, her eyes flickering to the television that Adam had left on. A chocolate-flavored cereal was being advertised by a benign-looking Dracula. "Oh, hi, Sunny." She switched off the TV with the remote control. "What's up?"

Never one for idle chitchat, Sunny launched directly into the reason for her call. "We've arranged another little demonstration at the research center. I thought you might like to come with me."

"Two days in a row? Don't you ever give it a rest?"

"Nope. Do you want to come?"

"Well, I don't know," Daphne hedged. "Adam didn't seem too thrilled to see me on the news last night and—"

"You mean to tell me you're going to let Adam, a man you're not even married to, dictate your conscience? Daphne Granger, I'm surprised at you."

"He's not dictating my conscience," Daphne defended the absent Adam loyally. "Actually, he didn't say a word about it."

"He doesn't have to," Sunny interjected. "I know him, he probably just *looked* at you with those big blue eyes of his, all disapproving and everything."

"Well, you're wrong. He didn't even do that. Besides—now don't be furious with me—but I'm not even sure I, uh, agree with what you're doing."

"Not agree!" Sunny was outraged. "How can you not agree that torturing innocent animals is wrong?"

"I don't know, Sunny. I mean, how else are doctors going to discover new cures?" she said, repeating the argument that both Brian and Adam had used. "They have to experiment somehow, don't they? And they certainly can't use people."

"So you wouldn't mind if they carved Mack up like a frog in biology class, is that what you're saying?"

Daphne sighed, exasperated. Sunny went right for the jugular when she was defending one of her causes. "Yes, of course I'd mind but that's not the point. Mack isn't going to end up in a research center like that. He—"

"How do you know? He could. What if he got lost and the pound picked him up?"

"I'd go down and get him."

"But what if you were out of town or something—" Sunny pressed on with single-minded zeal "—and couldn't get down there right away. Did you know that some pounds *sell* unclaimed animals to research labs?"

"No," Daphne said faintly. "I didn't know that."

"Well, there, you see!" Sunny pointed out triumphantly. "It *could* happen to Mack."

"Yes, I guess it could," Daphne admitted.

"So, are you just going to sit home and do nothing?"

"Well, I..."

"Hundreds of people's pets, cats just like Mack, are being slaughtered."

"Yes, but..." Oh, what the hell, she thought. *I haven't got anything better to do today. And it'll make Sunny happy.* "Okay, sure, pick me up."

"Good," Sunny said approvingly. "I knew I could count on you."

"NOW I KNOW WHY you're so good at fund raising," Daphne said, sitting beside Sunny in the yellow Mercedes as they drove to the research center. "Nobody would dare say no to you."

Sunny grinned unrepentantly. "Persistence has its uses."

"Intimidation, you mean."

"Who, *moi*?" Sunny's hand fanned out over her lush bosom as she gave Daphne a coy look.

"Yes, you!" Daphne said as they pulled to a stop across the street from the research center. "You ought to be ashamed of your strong-arm tactics."

"Why?" Sunny slammed the door and locked it. "They work don't they?" She grinned across the roof of the car. "You're here, aren't you?"

"Against my better judgment," Daphne admitted, following her friend across the street to the group marching in a tight circle in front of the center.

She recognized a few faces from the day before, Mollie's friend Jason among them, but there seemed to be more young people, more high school and college students, than there had been yesterday. Probably because it was a Saturday, Daphne thought. The mood was different, too. More unsettled and rambunctious, more... rebellious. But that, too, was to be expected, she decided philosophically. Teenagers were more excitable than young mothers with children.

Someone handed Daphne a sign and she took it automatically, holding her arm away from her body as Sunny tied a black armband around the sleeve of her jumpsuit.

The protesters were chanting loudly, thrusting their placards into the air with youthful zeal. As she took her place in line and began marching, Daphne noticed a squad car parked halfway down the street. There were two uniformed policemen sitting inside, silently watching the proceedings, just as they had been yesterday.

"Stop vivisection now!" the protesters chanted. "Vivisection is murdering our pets!"

Daphne marched halfheartedly, head down as she mumbled the words of the chant, and wondered how soon she could slip away without incurring Sunny's wrath. Giving in to Sunny's expert manipulations, she decided, had been a rotten, cowardly idea. She should have stayed home and watched cartoons.

The protesters continued to march, becoming louder and more rowdy with each passing minute. They began to jostle each other in their zeal. Daphne looked up from her morose contemplation of the cracks in the sidewalk. There was real anger in some of the faces around her; several pairs of eyes glowed with an idealistic fervor. This protest was more than just something to do on a Saturday afternoon for most of these people, Daphne realized, her eyes on the faces of those closest to her. To many of the young protesters this was obviously a "sacred crusade."

A twinge of uneasiness curled in her stomach and she glanced toward the parked police car. It was still there. One of the officers had gotten out of the car and was standing by the open door, radio in hand. Somewhat relieved by their reassuring presence, Daphne nevertheless scanned the crowd of angry protesters for Sunny. Police or not, she wanted to go home. Now!

Suddenly, someone hurled a brick through the front window of the research center. Glass went flying in every direction. Several people fell to the ground, protecting their heads with crossed arms. A woman screamed. Protest signs clattered to the sidewalk. A police siren blared.

Daphne's first instinct was to run. To drop her sign and join the scattering crowd as it fled for safety. But she couldn't move. She just stood there, frozen, feeling for a moment as if she had slipped back in time. Another brick sailed through the half-shattered window, flinging more glass, breaking the spell that held her captive. She started to turn away, looking for Sunny, when someone grabbed her wrist. The hold was not ungentle but not careful, either. She jerked away, startled, and dropped her sign.

"Come on now, lady. You don't want to add resisting arrest to the rest of it, do you?"

Cold steel clamped around her delicate wrist and Daphne looked up into the eyes of a uniformed policeman.

"But I didn't...I wasn't..." Her free hand gestured wildly as she tried to explain that she wasn't really involved. The policeman reached out, capturing it in his and, turning her expertly, cuffed her hands behind her back. "Now wait just a minute," she said, becoming frightened and, thus, angry. "I don't have anything to do with this. I was just—"

He gave her a little shove, urging her toward the police paddy wagon that had appeared on the scene. Another policeman stood by the open rear door, helping handcuffed protesters into the back.

"But I wasn't doing anything!" she said plaintively, looking up at him with wide frightened eyes as he took her elbow to assist her into the paddy wagon.

"Tell it to the judge," he said unsympathetically, turning away to assist the next prisoner.

Daphne fell back onto the hard bench seat, looking down at the floorboards in frightened bewilderment. *This can't be happening*, she thought wildly. She was all grown up now, an adult with a responsible, successful career. Things like this didn't happen to people like her!

Someone jostled her and she glanced up as Sunny, her hands cuffed behind her back, stumbled into the seat across from her.

The panic in her eyes receded. "This is all your fault," she hissed, fury in their golden depths.

"My fault?" Somehow, handcuffs and all, Sunny managed to look indignant. "*I* didn't throw that brick." She grinned suddenly. "But I'd sure like to thank whoever did."

"*What!*"

"I said I'd like to thank whoever did," she repeated.

Daphne couldn't believe her ears. "Why, for God's sake?"

"Just think of all the publicity," Sunny said gleefully. "And I didn't have to do a thing."

"Except get us both arrested," Daphne said nastily.

The door to the paddy wagon clanged shut and Daphne closed her eyes, head back against the cold metal side as she tried to digest the fact that she had actually been arrested. Her body jerked forward, bumping the person next to her, and then back again as the paddy wagon started to move.

Daphne's eyes flew open. "Oh, my God! The publicity!"

"What? What is it?" Sunny leaned forward, alarmed at the look on her friend's face.

"This is going to make the papers, isn't it? And the evening news?"

"I sure hope so."

A hysterical little laugh escaped her. "Adam is going to bust a gut," she said.

13

THE HANDCUFFS WERE REMOVED as soon as they got to the police station. Daphne rubbed her wrists, surprised there were no bruises, and looked around her with wide eyes.

She had only been in a police station once before, that time when she had tried to hit that TV cameraman over the head with her protest sign. She hadn't liked it then. She didn't like it now. The place was drab and depressing and frightening. It was crowded and too hot and it smelled from the press of too many bodies in too small a space.

Uniformed police officers moved through the throng of people, doing their jobs as efficiently as possible. Men and women in street clothes sat on the hard wooden benches smoking or drinking coffee or staring into space, looking scared or defiant or bored, depending on their temperament—and their reason for being there. A young woman in a too-short blue dress stood in front of the sergeant's desk, crying as she tried to explain something. And the newly arrived protesters milled around in a sort of helpless confusion, waiting to be told what to do.

"Hey, man, when do I get my phone call?" someone wanted to know.

"Just as soon as you've been booked."

"Yeah?" The questioner was a young man, intent on showing everybody just how scared he wasn't. "And when will that be?"

"Just as soon as we can get around to it," the policeman said, bored. "Now, all of you, find yourselves a seat over there somewhere and sit down. It's going to be a long day."

Daphne did as she was told, sitting down between Sunny and a little old man in a red beret who appeared to be sound asleep.

"God, this brings back memories, doesn't it?" Sunny said in her ear. Her tone was halfway between disgust and nostalgia.

"Ones I'd just as soon forget," Daphne said dryly.

"Yeah, now that you mention it..." Sunny's voice was confiding. "Me, too."

"How long do you think we'll be here?"

"I don't know. Hours probably." Sunny gestured with one hand, her dark red nails gleaming. "All these bodies to process through the system."

And it was hours. One by one, they were booked, searched, fingerprinted and photographed like common criminals. Daphne, standing stock-still as brisk, impersonal hands ran up and down her body, had never been so humiliated in her life. The charges, they were informed by the arresting officer, were disorderly conduct and criminal mischief, both misdemeanors. Then, finally, a judge arraigned them, setting bail at two hundred dollars apiece, payable they were told, in cash. No checks, no credit cards. Neither Daphne nor Sunny had that much on them.

"Now what happens?" Daphne asked hesitantly.

"You can call someone to come down with the money," an officer told her. "A family member or friend. Or you can call a bail bondsman. There's a phone book by the telephone there."

"And in the meantime?"

"In the meantime you wait in the tank."

The "tank" was segregated by sex, one for men, one for women. It was the worst place Daphne had ever been in her life. She hadn't experienced it during her one other brush with the law. That time, because it was her first offence and she had no record, the bail had been lower, and the organizers of the protest had been right there to pay it.

This time Daphne was made to suffer the indignity of having her valuables taken from her before she went into the tank. Her gold chains, her earrings, her watch and the contents of her pockets—a total of fifteen dollars and eighteen cents—were surrendered to the bored-looking officer behind the desk and sealed into little plastic bags that could be reclaimed, she was told, when she left the station.

And then, finally, the two women were allowed their phone call.

"I got hold of Brian," Sunny said. She sat down on the bench next to Daphne, huddling close as she looked around at the other occupants of the tank. "God, will you look at these women," she whispered, her brown eyes big as saucers. "Have you ever seen such a sorry-looking bunch of losers in your life?"

"Was he mad?"

"Who? Brian?" Sunny shuddered dramatically. "Are you kidding? I could feel the steam coming right through the telephone wire."

"But he's coming to get us, isn't he?" Daphne asked hopefully.

"He said he ought to let us stew for a while but, yes, he's coming to get us." She patted Daphne's hand comfortingly. "Are you sure you don't want to call Adam? You still have your one phone call."

Daphne shook her head. "I don't want to bother him at the hospital."

"He's probably not at the hospital anymore, Daphne. We've been in this hellhole since eleven-thirty this morning. That's—" she glanced down, forgetting that her watch had been surrendered to the desk sergeant "—well, several hours, anyway. He's probably home by now, and worried sick. You know what a worrier he is. Maybe you'd better take your one phone call and let him at least know where you are."

"I left a note taped to the refrigerator telling him I'd gone out with you for a little while."

"Oh, *that'll* put his mind at ease."

Brian arrived at the station forty minutes later. He wasn't nearly so angry as Sunny had indicated. In fact, he seemed to have cooled off enough to see the funny side of things. Adam, however, apparently didn't see anything funny in the situation at all.

"I didn't tell Brian to call him," Sunny whispered as the two women were led out of the holding tank. "Honest! Brian must have thought of it all by himself."

"Well, well, if it isn't the two little jailbirds," Brian said teasingly. But he took his wife in his arms and hugged her hard. "Are you all right?" he said against her hair.

"Fine, now that you're here," Sunny replied. Her voice was just the tiniest bit shaky as she clung to Brian, hiding her face in his shoulder for a moment.

Daphne wished she were being held, too. She would have enjoyed clinging to the security of Adam's broad shoulders, but Adam hadn't made the slightest move toward her. He just stood there, a somewhat wary expression on his face as he waited for her to claim her valuables. She surreptitiously studied the taut line of his mouth as she signed for the little plastic bag containing her possessions. He was, she thought, absolutely furious with her. She didn't blame him. She was furious with herself.

It was one thing to land in jail for a cause you believed in. And quite another to end up there for no good reason at all.

"Are you all right?" he asked when she came away from the desk. His voice was low, his words clipped.

"Yes, Adam," she said, head down. "Fine."

He reached out and lifted her chin with his forefinger, forcing her to look at him. "You're sure you're all right?" His eyes scanned her face for a brief, intense second or two, searching for heaven knew what. His expression was concerned and—for just a moment—fearful. "You're not hurt? We heard that there was broken glass."

"No," she said softly. Her hand came up to touch his. "I wasn't near the glass when it broke. I'm fine."

"Good." His hand dropped. "Then, shall we go?" he said tightly, putting his hand under her elbow to lead her out of the station.

"Yes, please." Sunny answered for both of them, curling her arm through Brian's as they headed for the door. "Let's get out of this place!"

They exited the police station to the glow of the late afternoon sunlight slanting across the pavement—and the flash of a newsman's camera exploding into their faces.

"What the hell—" Adam began, raising a hand to shield his face. He automatically drew Daphne closer, as if to shield her, too.

"Dr. McCorkle, how do you feel about your wife being involved in the antivivisection protest at the Hillman Medical Research Center?"

"No comment," Brian muttered, heading his wife toward the yellow Mercedes parked at the curb. Adam and Daphne crossed the pavement to the forest-green BMW parked right behind it.

"Dr. McCorkle, do you condone your wife's activities?" The reporter was persistent.

Designing Woman

Brian shook his head, still refusing to answer. He pulled open the car door and handed Sunny inside. She went quietly, kept silent by the look on her husband's face.

"Dr. McCorkle..."

The questions were still coming fast and furious, thrown at them from all sides by what seemed like dozens of reporters. In reality, there were only four. One of them, apparently, was just a little better informed than his colleagues. He aimed his question at Adam, who had not yet reached the safety of the car.

"Dr. Forrest, how does having your wife involved in a criminal protest against a medical research center affect your relatively new position at Children's Hospital? Do you think it will affect your career there?"

Daphne's eyes widened at that. She hadn't given a thought to how this might affect Adam. At least, not careerwise. After all, she wasn't his wife anymore and what she did should have no bearing on Adam's career. Even if she were his wife, it should have no bearing. She opened her mouth to correct the reporter's assumption. "I'm not Mrs.—" she began, but a hand clamped down on her arm, silencing her.

"We have no comment," Adam snapped, assisting Daphne into the passenger seat of his BMW. He slammed the door and stalked around the front of the car to the driver's side. Without a word, he inserted the key into the ignition and gunned the engine to life. And then careful, controlled, always-in-charge Adam left rubber on the road as he peeled away from the curb.

Daphne sat silently, unable to think of anything to say to defuse his anger. What could she say? "I'm sorry" was woefully inadequate. It was true, of course, but inadequate. "I didn't know what I was getting into" was true, too, but still no excuse. She *should* have known what she was getting into because anything was possible when Sunny McCorkle, master crusader, was involved.

"If I had known what Sunny was up to," she offered at last, "I wouldn't have gotten involved."

Adam didn't even glance at her. "A bit late for regrets, isn't it?" he said, downshifting as the car crested one of San Francisco's famous hills.

"I didn't say I *regretted* getting involved," Daphne snapped back, stung into saying something that she didn't mean by the abruptness of his comment. "I think it's a worthwhile cau—" The lie stuck in her throat. She didn't think it was a worthwhile cause at all. "Well, I'm sorry you had to get involved in the whole thing," she finished, eyes downcast as she plucked at the fabric of her jumpsuit.

"I suppose you'd rather I just left you sitting in jail? Would that have suited you better?"

"Brian would have bailed me out," she said, shrugging.

"Brian would not have bailed you out!" Adam exploded. He hit the steering wheel with the fist of his hand. "You're my responsibility!"

Daphne's head came up, all her senses ready—eager—to do battle. "I am not your responsibility," she said firmly, putting out a hand to brace herself against the dashboard as Adam turned onto their street. "I'm not anyone's responsibility."

"You're not even responsible for yourself!"

"Oh, really?" Her brows nearly disappeared into the wisps of hair on her forehead. "And who do you think has been taking care of me for the past several years? Santa Claus?"

"I wouldn't be the least bit surprised."

He swung the car into the driveway, bringing it to an abrupt halt only inches from the cream-colored paint of the garage door. Automatically, Daphne reached for the door handle, then stopped when she realized that Adam hadn't turned off the engine. "Do you intend to finish this—" she paused, searching for a word "—this *discussion* out here? In front of all your neighbors?"

"I don't want to finish it at all."

Daphne sat up straighter in her seat. "*You* don't want to finish it! Well, that's just too bad, Dr. Forrest, because I do."

"Fine. Finish it on your own. I have to go back to the hospital." He revved the engine as if to emphasize his impatience to be off.

"Oh, that's right!" Daphne said, her voice low and fierce with the effort to keep from shrieking at the top of her lungs. "Run off to the hospital whenever life gets a little too real for you. Hide behind your white coat. Well, I've got news for you, doctor. Your problems will still be waiting for you when you get back," she informed him icily, shoving the car door open.

He turned his head toward her. "Will they?" he said, very softly.

For just a moment Daphne hesitated, caught by the look on his face. It was hopeful and worried at the same time. She almost said something soothing, but then she realized the car was still running, that Adam's foot was still revving the gas pedal, and the moment vanished.

"Count on it!" she shouted, springing out of the car before he could say another word. She slammed the door as hard as she could then turned and flounced across the yard into the house. Tires squealed as Adam backed out of the driveway and roared off down the street. "Damn the man!" she cursed aloud, wishing she had something to throw. "He hasn't changed a bit!"

Oh, he was older, smoother, more expert with words of love. No, not love, she thought, her expression suddenly vicious. *Seduction.* He knew all the right words to say when he had her in his arms. But when it came to emotion—real, honest, heartfelt emotion—he was as closemouthed as ever. Be it love or hate or anger, he couldn't say the words. Couldn't tell her what was in his heart.

Well, *that* was coming to an end! And soon. Very soon. She would wait until he cooled off, until he wasn't so blazingly angry. And then she would confront him with her feelings, all of them, and demand that he expose his own. If she had to hold him down and sit on him, she would know what he really felt. There would be no more pussy-footing around the edges of this relationship of theirs. If it was love, the real, committed, ending-in-marriage, forever kind of love, she wanted to know. And if it was just a sexual fling...well, she wanted to know that, too. She couldn't go on like this, not knowing. It would drive her crazy before very much longer.

Somewhat calmer now that she had made a decision, she walked through the deserted house to the bedroom, shrugging out of her jumpsuit as she went. It felt soiled; dirtied by the hands that had run so impersonally over her when the police officer had "patted her down" looking for God knew what.

In the bedroom she kicked off her shoes, letting the jumpsuit slide down her legs to the floor. She stepped out of it and then, remembering she was trying to be more tidy, bent over to pick it up. The kitten, Tiger, wound his way between her feet, asking for attention.

Daphne scratched behind his ears. "What's the matter, little fella? The other guys desert you?"

"Meow," said Tiger piteously, rubbing against her hand.

Daphne straightened, tossing the jumpsuit over her arm. "Yeah, I know just what you mean," she said, carrying the soiled garment with her to the bathroom. She dropped it on top of the wicker clothes hamper and reached into the shower to turn on the taps. Her jumpsuit wasn't all that felt dirty after her little run-in with the law.

The phone was ringing as she stepped out of the shower. For a moment, she considered not answering it. It might be Adam. But, she decided, he knew she was here. And there was no sense in making him any madder than he already was. Besides, maybe he had chosen the phone as a way of apologizing. *Fat chance*, her mind sneered as she reached for the receiver.

"Hello?"

"Thank goodness I finally got you." Elaine sounded breathless and exasperated. "I've been calling all afternoon. *Where* have you been?"

Daphne hitched her towel a little more securely around her damp body. "Believe me. You don't want to know." She sighed, sinking down on the bed. "So—" her voice became businesslike and professional "—what's the problem?"

"Mr. Chan is here *now* and he's leaving tomorrow night. And he wants to see you. I told him you'd—"

"What happened to our Monday meeting?" Daphne interrupted her new business partner.

"His oldest grandson is having surgery on Tuesday—or is it Wednesday? Anyway, he wants to be back with him for that. Which means he's here now, two days ahead of schedule."

"Can't you handle it?" Daphne inquired. "You're a partner."

"I told him that, Daphne. But he insists on seeing you. You know how he is about dealing with the 'head man.'"

"Yes, I know." Daphne fell silent for a moment, thinking. Mr. Chan had the worst timing in the world! She needed to be *here* right now, dealing with Adam and the rest of her life. But business was business. And Mr. Chan was there about the fabrics for her new lingerie line. She needed to see him now, too, if the line was going to launch on schedule. Damn!

"Daphne, you there?"

"Yes." Her voice was resigned.

"You flying out?"

For a moment more Daphne struggled with what she should do and what she wanted to do. "Yes," she said, her sense of responsibility winning out. Besides, maybe two or three days would given Adam the time he needed to really cool off. "Yes, I'm flying out."

Rapidly, now that her decision was made, she began to plan. "Have someone meet the next San Francisco plane at La Guardia. Unless you hear otherwise, I'll be on it. And send a basket of fruit to Mr. Chan's suite with my—*our*—compliments. And make reservations at someplace fancy for dinner tomorrow night for three." She ripped a piece of paper off the telephone notepad and began scribbling. "Yes. You, me and Mr. Chan. It's high time he got used to dealing with someone other than me. No, I don't, but you can have your secretary call his secretary and find out what his favorite place is. Oh, and would you please make sure there's enough food for a couple of days in my apartment? Nothing fancy, just something to keep me alive for a day or two. I'll be coming right back." She paused a moment, listening. "Let's not go into that now, okay? We'll discuss it when I get there. Yes. Bye."

Daphne pressed down on the telephone button, breaking the connection with New York, and dialed the airlines. After making reservations on the next flight into La Guardia, she called a taxi and then hurried to the bathroom and finished putting herself together.

In less than twenty minutes she was dressed in trim ankle-length slacks and a matching unlined jacket in a nubby beige fabric with a russet-colored string knit sweater beneath it. Large copper discs adorned her ears, a long oblong silk scarf in shades of brown, beige and peach was looped under the lapels of her jacket, and flat strappy sandals in deep tobacco-brown were on her narrow feet. She stuffed a few essentials into a large leather-and-canvas carryall and headed for Adam's den to write a note.

While dressing, she had debated whether or not to call him instead, and calmly, rationally explain the situation. But just thinking of his thundercloud of a face put her right off that idea. A note, she decided, was the safest bet. Cowardly, but safe. He should be good and cooled off by the time he got home and read it. If she called the hospital to explain, he might still be mad. Or she might be interrupting something, which would make him mad all over again. A note would be better.

As she was writing it, she heard the front door open. Apparently, she thought, the decision had been taken out of her hands. She wondered if that were good or bad. "I'm in here, Adam," she called, resigned to meeting him head-on.

There was no answer.

Daphne came out of the den, her carryall over one shoulder, the note in her other hand. "I was just writing you a note," she explained. "I know it's terrible timing but Elaine called and I have to fly out to New..." Her voice trailed off as she saw who it was. "Oh, hello, Marcia," she said coolly, inclining her head toward the younger woman. They had silently agreed to a truce of sorts; not a friendly one by any means but at least there were no outright hostilities. "I'm afraid Adam's not home right now. He had an emergency at the hospital."

"Yes, I know *exactly* what kind of emergency Adam had. It's all over the hospital that he had to go down to the police station and bail out his ex-wife!"

"Oh, dear," Daphne said, sincerely sorry and sincerely distressed. Above almost anything else in life, Adam valued his professional image. Quite rightly, too, she thought, since he had worked so hard to attain it. He wouldn't look kindly on anyone who smudged it for him. Of course, what she had done should have had no bearing on Adam. But would he look at it that way? It was easy to see that Marcia didn't. Like sister, like brother, she thought.

"Is that all you can say? 'Oh, dear'?" Adam's sister scoffed. "Not that I expected anything better of you after what Adam's told me." She advanced on Daphne like a lioness all set to defend her cub, although she made no overt move to inflict bodily harm.

It was the look in her eyes, Daphne decided. If looks could kill...

"I *told* him you'd be nothing but trouble! I told him that you hadn't changed. That you still had the same crazy, radical friends and believed in the same stupid causes. I told him you were no better doctor's wife material now than you were the first time around. And you've proved it." A particularly nasty, rather triumphant smile curved her pink lips. "*Now* maybe he'll listen to me."

"Maybe," Daphne agreed softly, her voice as level and calm as she could make it as she digested the rather disturbing fact that Adam had obviously discussed their relationship with his viper of a sister. Old tight-lipped Adam, who wouldn't even discuss his feelings with her, had discussed them with his sister. How dare he! Their relationship, however it turned out, was private. Silently, she added another bone to the pile she had to pick with Dr. Adam Forrest when she got back from New York.

"Maybe?" Marcia's voice rose to a near shriek. With a visible effort, she controlled it. "Oh, he'll listen all right. He can't help but listen with the evidence right in front of his eyes."

"Maybe," Daphne said again. She brushed past Marcia and went into the kitchen to tape her note to the refrigerator door, crumpling her earlier one—the one that had told him she had gone out with Sunny—in her hand. "That's something we'll have to discuss when I get back." She glanced over her shoulder, eyebrows raised as she gave Marcia a deliberately arch look. "Adam and I, that is." She paused consideringly. "Although, if what you say is true, I'm sure Adam will let you know what we decide."

A horn sounded outside, three sharp blasts piercing the air.

Daphne silently blessed the efficiency of the San Francisco taxi companies. "That will be my cab," she said, heading for the front door with barely concealed relief. She paused with her hand on the knob. "Feel free to make yourself at home until Adam gets back. I'm sure he won't be long. And I'm sure you'll have plenty to say to him," she finished sweetly, and left.

14

"MRS. GRANGER." Elaine's young assistant hurried into the workroom, her expression agitated, her manner flustered. "Mrs. Granger, there's a man in the lobby. He insists on seeing you and he ... he's *drunk!*"

"I am not drunk," corrected Adam, coming into the workroom behind the young woman. "I have been drinking," he said. "Two brandies, to be precise. The second of which the flight attendant spilled all over my jacket."

Daphne just stared. Never, ever, had she seen Adam in this condition. Maybe he wasn't drunk, she thought, but he certainly looked it. His golden hair was falling every which way, his cheeks and chin were heavy with the stubble of a day's growth, and she would have sworn under oath that he was wearing the same clothes he had put on yesterday morning for their canceled picnic. They looked as if he had slept in them.

"Adam, what are you doing here?" She rose to her feet behind her littered worktable, truly alarmed. Adam all undone like this was a frightening sight. She couldn't imagine what could have happened to make him lose his cool like this. "What's wrong?"

"You're what's wrong," he said, coming toward her with purposeful strides. He maneuvered around the worktable with ease, not even glancing at the half-clad model who stood draped in little more than a length of lavender silk.

Daphne shrank back from the murderous look in his eyes. "Me?" she squeaked, casting about in her mind for what she might have done to put that expression in his face. Suddenly, Marcia's words came back with great clarity. *It's all over the hospital that he had to go down to the police station and bail out his ex-wife.* No, she thought, surely he couldn't be this mad about that. Not mad enough to come all the way to New York without even taking the time to change his clothes. Oh, God, she thought, it must have made the papers! No wonder he looked mad enough to kill.

"Yes, you!" He rounded the worktable and grabbed her by the upper arms, completely oblivious to the four grinning women and one puzzled Chinese man who stood gaping at them. "You've run out on me for the last time. Is that clear, Daffy?" He shook her for emphasis. "The very last time! Do you understand me?"

"No, Adam, I don't. I—"

"The last time, Daffy," he repeated, his voice low and more than a little threatening. "I won't let you do this to me again."

"Do *what* to you again?"

"*Leave me!*" He practically shouted the words into her startled face.

"Leave you? I haven't left you, Adam. I had a meeting with Mr. Chan that couldn't be put off. I was coming right back."

But Adam wasn't listening. "You *left* me," he went on angrily. "*Again*. Without so much as a goodbye. Without even a goddamn note to tell me where you'd gone."

"But I left you a note. I—"

"Without a note!" he roared, his voice overpowering hers. "I came home from the hospital determined to have it out with you and what do I find? Nothing, that's what I find!" he said furiously. "You said you'd still be there when I got back. 'Count on it,' you said. But you weren't there." He shook his head as if he still found that fact hard to grasp.

"At first, I thought you'd gone out for a while. Taken a walk to cool off. Your clothes were still there. The cats hadn't been fed. I was sure you wouldn't run off without taking care of the cats first. But you didn't come back." His voice broke slightly and he let go of her, turning away as he ran a hand through his already tousled hair. "I called Sunny but she hadn't heard from you...so I began to think all sorts of things. That you'd been mugged. Raped. God knows what." He turned back to her, blue eyes blazing like an avenging angel's. "I had to find out from Marcia that you'd gone back to New York. You were too much of a coward to tell me yourself."

"Marcia?" Daphne said, stunned. "What does Marcia have to do with—" And then it hit her. Obviously Marcia had destroyed her note. "That bitch!"

Adam grabbed her by the shoulders again. "You leave my sister out of this, do you hear me?" He shook her again to make sure that she did. "This is between you and me."

Daphne wrenched herself out of his hands, furious herself now. Neither one of them spared a thought for their fascinated audience. "Don't you yell at me!" she shouted. "Yell at that interfering sister of yours. She's the one who—"

"Oh, that's right, blame it on someone else." Adam threw up his hands. "Don't take responsibility for your own actions."

"*My* own actions! It's Marcia who—"

"Marcia, hell! It's *you* who ran off at the first sign of trouble, *you* who couldn't face up to what you had done."

"What I had done?" Daphne was red-faced with righteous indignation. "I haven't done anything."

"Huh!" Adam's sneer was eloquent. "Just landed yourself in jail with a bunch if idealistic, knot-headed teenagers."

"It was for a good cause!" Daphne defended herself, forgetting in the heat of the moment that good cause though it might be, it wasn't a cause she believed in.

"I don't care how good a cause it is. That's beside the point."

"And just what is the point, Dr. Forrest?" Daphne inquired nastily.

"You want to know what the point is?" Adam advanced until they were standing nose to nose. Daphne refused to back down. "The point is you." He jabbed a forefinger into her chest for emphasis. "Why the hell can't you act like a reasonable adult instead of some flaky, irresponsible hippie who goes running off at the first sign of trouble?"

"I was never a hippie! You just thought so because you were always such a pompous stuffed shirt. Old, dedicated, tight-lipped Adam, who wouldn't know an honest emotion if it walked up and bit him. And I did not run away!" she added furiously. "You divorced *me*, remember?" she reminded him angrily, slipping back in time without missing a beat. "And you haven't changed one bit. You still put your precious career ahead of everything else, even—"

"*I* haven't changed? You're the one who hasn't changed," Adam roared, grabbing her by the shoulders again. "I'm willing to compromise and—"

"Even love," Daphne continued as if Adam hadn't spoken. She was so caught up in airing past grievances that his words didn't even register. "Oh, I should have known it wouldn't work," she cried, slipping back into the present as easily as she had slipped out of it. "I don't know what made me think it would. I guess I just wanted it so much that I didn't think the situation through. But, then, according to you, I never think anything through. I guess that's just another example of—"

Adam clamped her shoulders tighter. "I want it, too!" he shouted, cutting off her words.

"Want what?" Daphne shouted back, busy trying to squirm out of his grasp. But Adam's hands, his skillful surgeon's hands, were strong as well as gentle and he held her fast.

"You! I want you to come back to me."

Daphne went very, very still. "Why?" she demanded, asking the question as if her life depended on it.

"Because you're my wife!"

Daphne shook her head stubbornly. "Not anymore."

"Then because I love you, dammit!" he bellowed.

Daphne's mouth fell open. It wasn't the way she had envisioned him saying he loved her. But he *had* said it. And it was the sweetest, most wonderful thing she had ever heard. Her eyes misted, her throat closing over the words that clamored to be said. Words she had been waiting to say for eleven long years. "Oh, Adam," she whispered instead. "Adam." It was the only word she seemed able to say. It was enough.

Adam slid his hands from her shoulders to her back, enfolding her in a tentative embrace. "And because you love me, too," he said softly, lowering his head. He hesitated a moment before kissing her, his eyes hopeful and just a tiny bit afraid. "Don't you?"

"Oh, Adam." Daphne threw her arms around his neck and pulled his head the rest of the way down to hers. "Oh, Adam, you fool. Yes!" she said against his lips, punctuating her words with quick little kisses. "Yes, yes, yes."

His mouth came down on hers then, abruptly stopping the joyous flow of words. He pulled her more firmly to his body, his arms hard around her, his eyes glistening with unshed tears of happiness. Their lips touched...and parted...and touched again.

"I love you," he whispered into her mouth, his hands firm and warm against her back.

"I love you," she echoed, as she tangled her fingers in his tousled hair. She pulled his head closer, demanding more.

Their mouths touched again and clung. Lips and tongues tasting, testing, cherishing. Both of them physically affirming the words they had just said aloud.

"Way 'ta go, Gorgeous!" Elaine's voice, brimming with laughter, urged them on.

Adam raised his head a fraction and looked around. Four beaming female faces, and one very puzzled male one, were watching them with avid interest. Adam blushed, the color rising swiftly from the open throat of his sportshirt to his hairline.

Spontaneously, the women burst into applause. Mr. Chan, not wanting to do the incorrect thing, joined them.

Daphne grinned happily and executed a sketchy little bow. She was practically jerked off her feet as Adam's big hand closed around her wrist. "Elaine, you're in charge," he said, dragging Daphne toward the door.

"But Mr. Chan..." Daphne sputtered, but she wasn't really objecting.

"I'll take care of him." Elaine slipped her arm through Mr. Chan's. "We'll get along just fine, won't we?" she said, patting his hand.

Mr. Chan smiled tentatively and bowed.

"You go with Gorgeous," Elaine ordered, nodding approvingly as Adam continued to drag her business partner across the room.

Having no choice—and wanting none—Daphne went.

"AND YOU'D REALLY THOUGHT I'd left you for good?"

"Really." Adam finished lathering up his hands and reached beneath the water for her foot. Holding her heel in one hand, he began to massage the floral-scented soap over her arch and between her toes. "What else was I supposed to think?" he asked. "I come home to an empty house. Three hungry cats, begging to be fed. No Daphne. No note." He ran his hand up over the swell of her calf and back down again. "No nothing."

"I already explained to you about that."

"Yes," he said. He put her left foot down and picked up the other one. "I intend to have a little heart-to-heart with my baby sister when we get back."

"Don't be too hard on her, Adam," Daphne advised, feeling magnanimous and forgiving with Adam sitting at the other end of her bathtub, doing deliciously sensuous things to her feet. "She was only trying to save you from yourself." She grinned wickedly and wiggled her toes under the water. "And me."

Adam grinned back. That slow, sleepy, utterly sexy grin that turned her bones to mush. If she wasn't already half lying down she would have melted. As it was, she sank another few inches into the mountain of perfumed bubbles.

"I don't want to be saved from you, Daffy," he said softly, sincerely. "I never did."

"Never?"

"Never," Adam said solemnly.

"Not even the first time around?"

"Not even then."

"Then why—Oh, that feels wonderful." She sighed and fell silent a moment, enjoying the feel of his strong, gentle hands caressing her foot, and almost forgetting her question. "Why did you file for divorce?" she finally asked. It was an old issue, an old hurt, better off forgotten, but she needed to know the answer. And, despite the lightness of her tone, the old hurt showed through.

Adam stopped caressing her foot, placing the sole against his bare, hairy chest. "I don't know exactly," he said, trying to answer honestly. "I was angry. And—" he groped for a word "—hurt, I guess."

"Hurt? What had I done to hurt you?"

"You left me," he stated simply. "To follow your career."

Daphne pulled herself upright and her foot slid down his stomach into the water. "But it was only going to be for a couple of months! I was coming back. You knew I was coming back!"

"I know but..." He shrugged and ran his index finger up and down her shin. He looked for all the world like a small boy admitting to something that embarrassed him beyond words. "I couldn't have left you, Daffy. Not for any length of time at all. Not for any reason. And it hurt like hell to think that you could leave me."

"Oh, Adam." Daphne leaned forward, her movement causing little ripples of water and bubbles to lap against his chest as she reached out to touch him. "Why didn't you say something? Why didn't you tell me how you felt instead of getting all macho and *ordering* me not to go? We could have worked something out."

He shrugged again, still not looking at her. "Pride, I guess. If you didn't want to stay, I wasn't going to beg you to."

"But you filed for divorce. If you felt the way you say, why—" her hand slithered up his wet arm and she touched his cheek, urging him to look at her "—why did you file for divorce if you loved me?" she said, truly puzzled. "I don't understand."

"I don't really understand it, either," Adam admitted. He pressed her palm to his cheek with his hand, but his eyes were still shuttered against her, focused on the froth of iridescent bubbles that floated on the surface of the water. "But at the time, well, it seemed to make perfect sense. I was young and angry and stupid. And so crazy in love with you that I wasn't thinking straight. I had some half-baked idea that filing for divorce would bring you back to me. That if you really loved me, you'd come back and fight it." His eyes lifted to hers briefly and then dropped, but not quickly enough to hide the old hurts that still haunted him. "When you didn't, I thought, well . . . that you'd decided you didn't love me after all. That your career was more important than I was."

"Oh, no, Adam! How could you think that? I loved you then like I love you now." She moved forward until she was kneeling between his thighs and took his face in her hands, forcing him to look at her. Water sloshed over the edge of the tub, soaking the bright tangerine carpet, but neither of them noticed it. "I loved you passionately. With all my heart and soul. When you filed for divorce I thought you didn't love *me!*"

"Not love you. Daffy, that's crazy."

"It's not crazy!" She reared back and slapped the water with her hand, sending bubbles flying. "What else was I supposed to think? You didn't want to marry me in the first place and—"

"You were so young," Adam said, defending himself. "I didn't want to push you into something you'd regret later."

"Push me!" Daphne sank back on her heels, incredulity written all over her face. Her breasts swayed with the movement, tiny bubbles clinging to their rounded slopes, drops of water glistening on their tips. "I practically had to blackmail you into marriage. How could you think you were pushing me?"

"Because I wanted it..." He licked his lips, his eyes suddenly caught by her swaying breasts. "Wanted you so much that I *didn't* think. I just felt. And what I was feeling was driving me crazy." He looked up, catching her eyes, and grinned slowly. "Just like it's driving me crazy now."

But Daphne wasn't paying any attention. "But that doesn't make any sense," she said indignantly. "You didn't want to marry me because you loved me. You divorced me because you loved me. You... *Adam!*"

Adam had reached out, cupping his warm wet hands under her breasts. He slid his palms to her sides, his thumbs resting under the lower curve of her breasts, his fingers curling toward her back.

"Adam, I'm trying to talk to you," she said, putting her hands on his shoulders. Her elbows were stiff, holding him off.

He shook his head. "No more talking."

"But we're not finished discussing this," Daphne insisted.

"Yes, we are. It's yesterday's news. Over. And what matters now is *now*—and the rest of our lives."

"But I need to ask you one more question."

"All right." His thumbs feathered up the undersides of her breasts and flickered across her nipples. "Ask. I'm listening."

"You are not. You're—" She gasped as his thumbs brushed her nipples again. "I can't talk when you do that. I can't even *think* when you do that."

His hands tightened, pulling her to him as he slid down into the water. Bubbles teased at his chin. "Good," he murmured, satisfaction evident in his deep tones.

Daphne let herself be pulled forward until she was lying on top of Adam, her breasts resting high on his chest, her bare bottom poking out of the bubbles like twin moons. But she wouldn't let him kiss her. Not yet.

"I still have one question," she insisted, holding him off.

"Now?" He ran his hand along the curve of her spine, smoothing it all the way down to the swell of her exposed buttocks.

"Yes." Daphne's voice faltered only slightly. "Now."

"But—"

"No." She put a finger on his lips, silencing the rest of his protest. "No 'buts,' Adam. That's how we got into trouble the last time. We made love instead of talking things out."

Her chin tilted stubbornly. "I'm not going to let that happen to us again."

Adam's hand stilled on her back. "You're right," he said, resigned. "Ask your question."

Suddenly, Daphne didn't know quite where to start. "Well, I... that is..." Surprising herself, Daphne blushed. She looked down, her eyes following the path of her finger as it curved down his neck and out across his shoulder.

"Daphne?" Adam said, his curiosity more than a little piqued now.

"I... Oh, never mind." She shrugged, suddenly feeling silly to have made such an issue of what was, after all, really nothing. "It isn't important, anyway."

"No, I won't 'never mind,'" he insisted. "If you've still got a question about us, it's important. Ask it."

"Well, it's just that you've been so... Oh, damn! This isn't going to come out right, especially after what just went on in that bedroom in there."

What had 'gone on in that bedroom' was loving so abandoned, so uncontrolled, so intensely emotional that Daphne wondered how she could ever have thought that Adam was holding anything back. Assured of her love, he had given everything to her—his body, his thoughts, his very soul. And she, freed by his lack of constraint, had given him all of her.

"Come on," Adam prompted, a soft sexy smile curving his lips as he remembered their loving. "What have I been?"

Daphne's blush deepened. "You've been so, well, so standoffish with me these past six weeks. So distant."

She felt, rather than heard, the rumble of his laughter beneath her breasts. "Standoffish? Are you kidding?" Adam chuckled. "You call *this* standoffish? When I've practically ravished you every time we got within two feet of each other?" He grinned wickedly. "Not to mention what 'just went on in that bedroom.'"

Daphne's eyebrows rose into the damp tendrils of hair clinging to her forehead. "That isn't what I mean and you know it."

"Then what did you mean?"

"Well, you've been so cool. So damn *tolerant*. Now stop laughing!" She reared back slightly and punched his shoulder. "I'm serious."

Adam arranged his face into properly serious lines.

Daphne settled back against his chest, squishing bubbles between them. "What I mean is," she began again, toying with his hair. "Well, why didn't you get mad when I appeared on the evening news in Sunny's protest march? And why didn't you get upset when I left junk all over your nice clean house. And—"

Adam put a finger on her lips. "I think I get the picture," he said, smiling when Daphne closed her teeth around its tip and bit lightly. "I didn't get upset for the same reason, I suspect, that you didn't get upset when I had to stay late at the hospital, or when I was called back after we'd already settled in for the night. Compromise," he stated succinctly. "Neither one of us wanted to make the other angry. And, I think, we were trying to show each other just how much we'd changed. At least, I was."

"Hmm," Daphne said, digesting this. It was amazingly close to her own line of reasoning. "But you were so angry when you came down to the police station to bail me out. You were furious, in fact. What happened to the compromise then?"

"That wasn't anger, Daffy. Well, not all of it, anyway. It was fear. Stark terror. You weren't home when I got back from the hospital."

"But I left a note that time," she reminded him.

He gave her a wry look. "Telling me you'd gone out with Sunny 'for a little while.' I thought you'd gone stomping out in a huff because I'd had to cancel our picnic."

"But I wasn't in a huff at all. I understood why you had to rush off to the hospital. Really."

"I know. I know. But that's what I thought. And then your 'little while' stretched into a couple of hours and I began to get angry. Then it turned into all day and I started to worry, too." He sighed, remembering. "When Brian called to tell me that you and Sunny had been arrested that was the last straw." He placed his hands around her throat. "I was just about ready to wring your lovely neck."

"So," Daphne crowed. "You *were* mad."

"Furious," he admitted easily, his thumbs stroking the sides of her throat. "And terrified that I'd blow up and we'd end up arguing." He shuddered and his hands drifted to her shoulders. "And you know what happened the last time we argued."

"Same thing as always. We ended up in bed, making up."

"That's what I thought, too," he said, shaking his head. "But you're right about what you said before, Daffy. We never really did make up, we just postponed the arguments for a while."

Silently, Daphne nodded her agreement.

"But the last time we argued, it—" his voice got very quiet, very solemn "—it was eleven years before I saw you again."

"Oh, no, Adam! It wasn't the argument that kept us apart. It was—"

"I know," he said quietly, his hands soothing her back. "Intellectually, I know—knew," he corrected himself. "I knew that. But it didn't help. I was still afraid that it would happen all over again. That, if we argued, you'd leave. When I got home last night and you were gone I thought it *had* happened again."

"But it wasn't the arguing that drove us apart all those years ago," she said, determined to make him see. "It was the silence. If we had really argued...really discussed things and gotten everything out in the open it would have been okay, don't you see?"

"Yes, I do see. I really do. And from now on..." His hands tightened on her back for just a second. "From now on, we'll talk things out. No matter what. Agreed?"

"Agreed," she echoed softly, her eyes shining golden.

"Good!" He grinned suddenly, deliberately lightening the mood. "Because if you didn't agree, I'd just have to drag you back by the hair."

"Oh, really?"

"Yes, really. I'll have you know I was fully prepared for a knock-down drag-out fight. Physical, verbal...whatever it took to get you to come back to me."

"After two brandies," Daphne reminded him, an impish look on her face.

"Actually, I had those brandies on the plane, *after* I'd decided to come after you." His hands swooped down her back again, his palms curving over her wet silky rump. "Speaking of which, do you think I'll ever be able to get the smell out of my clothes?"

"We won't know for a while."

"Oh, why not?"

"They won't be back from the cleaners until tomorrow."

"You mean I'm without clothes until tomorrow?"

"Uh-huh. Not a stitch." She smiled seductively. "Except, of course, for a very sexy pair of black silk underwear."

"Don't you think we ought to take advantage of that?" he suggested. His hands slipped lower, his fingers curling around the backs of her thighs.

"Of what? The underwear?"

"If you like." Adam gave a little tug on her thighs, bringing her a bit higher on his body. Daphne's knees bent at the urging of his hands, coming to rest on either side of his hips. "But I was thinking of something just a little more basic." He bumped his pelvis against hers, causing water to slosh against the sides of the tub. "What do you say?" he murmured, lifting his mouth toward hers.

"I say yes," she answered, lowering her head to meet him halfway.

Harlequin Temptation

COMING NEXT MONTH

#105 THE SKY'S THE LIMIT
Jill Bloom

Charlotte could navigate a plane around the world, yet she couldn't chart a steady course with Bobby. She needed a friend, a kindred spirit, a mechanic.... Did she need a lover, too?

#106 AFTER THE RAIN
Madeline Harper

Emma Dixon's foray into the jungles of the Yucatán was not without incident. Adventure and intrigue followed fast on her heels—as did the attractive and virile Jack Winston.

#107 HOOK, LINE AND SINKER
Lynn Turner

Turning city slicker Travis McCauley into a fisherman and all-round nature boy was a challenge Mica couldn't resist. He'd brought his own very special lures....

#108 CAPTIVATED
Carla Neggers

He had style; she had nerve. Together Richard and Sheridan were winners in a real-life cops and robbers game. Their biggest gamble was with each other....

Just what the woman on the go needs!

BOOKMATE

The perfect "mate" for all Harlequin paperbacks!

Holds paperbacks open for hands-free reading!

- TRAVELING
- VACATIONING
- AT WORK • IN BED
- COOKING • EATING
- STUDYING

Perfect size for all standard paperbacks, this wonderful invention makes reading a pure pleasure! Ingenious design holds paperback books OPEN and FLAT so even wind can't ruffle pages—leaves your hands free to do other things. Reinforced, wipe-clean vinyl-covered holder flexes to let you turn pages without undoing the strap...supports paperbacks so well, they have the strength of hardcovers!

Snaps closed for easy carrying.

Available now. Send your name, address, and zip or postal code, along with a check or money order for just $4.99 + .75¢ for postage & handling (for a total of $5.74) payable to Harlequin Reader Service to:

Harlequin Reader Service
901 Fuhrmann Blvd.
P.O. Box 1325
Buffalo, N.Y. 14269

Offer not available in Canada.

Take 4 books & a surprise gift FREE

SPECIAL LIMITED-TIME OFFER

Mail to **Harlequin Reader Service®**

In the U.S.
901 Fuhrmann Blvd.
P.O. Box 1394
Buffalo, N.Y. 14240-1394

In Canada
P.O. Box 2800, Station "A"
5170 Yonge Street
Willowdale, Ontario M2N 6J3

YES! Please send me 4 free Harlequin Temptation® novels and my free surprise gift. Then send me 4 brand-new novels every month as they come off the presses. Bill me at the low price of $1.99 each — a 13% saving off the retail price. There are no shipping, handling or other hidden costs. There is no minimum number of books I must purchase. I can always return a shipment and cancel at any time. Even if I never buy another book from Harlequin, the 4 free novels and the surprise gift are mine to keep forever.

142-BPX-BP6S

Name _____ (PLEASE PRINT) _____

Address _____ Apt. No. _____

City _____ State/Prov. _____ Zip/Postal Code _____

This offer is limited to one order per household and not valid to present subscribers. Price is subject to change.

DOHT-SUB-1R

Harlequin Intrigue

Because romance can be quite an adventure.

Available wherever paperbacks are sold or through

Harlequin Reader Service

In the U.S.
901 Fuhrmann Blvd.
P.O. Box 1325
Buffalo, N.Y. 14269

In Canada
P.O. Box 2800, Station "A"
5170 Yonge Street
Willowdale, Ontario M2N 6J3

INT-6R

Now Available!
Buy all three books in MAURA SEGER'S fabulous trilogy!

EYE OF THE STORM

ECHO OF THUNDER

EDGE OF DAWN

Be a part of the Callahan and Gargano families as they live and love through the most turbulent decades in history!

"...should be required reading for every American."
— *Romantic Times*

To order all three books please send your name, address and zip or postal code along with a check or money order for $12.15 (includes 75¢ for postage and handling) made payable to Worldwide Library Reader Service to:

WORLDWIDE LIBRARY READER SERVICE

In the U.S.:	In Canada:
P.O. Box 1397	5770 Yonge St., P.O. Box 2800
Buffalo, N.Y.	Postal Station A
14240-1397	Willowdale, Ontario M2N 6J3

PLEASE SPECIFY BOOK TITLES WITH YOUR ORDER.

TRL-H-1